Shadows of Quartz

by

Nicholas Milano

Gem Haven Series, Volume 2

Shadows of Quartz

Cover Art by *Debbie Taylor*

The Wild Rose Press, Inc.
PO Box 708
Adams Basin, NY 14410-0708
Visit us at www.thewildrosepress.com

Publishing History
First Fantasy Rose Edition, 2017
Print ISBN 978-1-5092-1336-8
Digital ISBN 978-1-5092-1337-5

Gem Haven Series, Volume 2
Published in the United States of America

The shadows around John stopped moving, frozen in time, and turned on him, bombarding him with images, thoughts, and memories.

"I'm not weak." Mark whimpered.

"Follow the stars," an old woman said.

"Help me!" A young girl with auburn hair cried out. John reached for her, but she slipped away replaced by another nightmare.

"You can't stop me, I will rise again!" said a shrouded figure, his voice powerful and dark. *Igneous.* The figures sped toward the pillar.

John, trapped under the weight of the shadows, couldn't make any sense of the images speeding past.

"Wake up," Milo demanded.

John woke in a cold sweat, twisted in a pile of damp hotel bed sheets. Images flashed like distant memories already fading away.

The bed beside his own? Empty. This marked the third night in a row Milo sneaked off after John fell asleep. Igneous' attack had left a mark on each of them, especially Milo.

The full moon outside left a blue cast in his room for the past week. It wasn't real. What was?

Praise for Nicholas Milano

"I was pulled right in to the book and was able to feel and see every character! I am on pins and needles waiting for the next adventure!"

~Jamylynn Simmons

Dedication

This book is dedicated to my parents,
who convinced me to follow my dream
of being a writer,
but mostly as a hobby.

Chapter One

Dreams are where you go when you want to escape from reality, but where do you go when you want to escape from your dreams?

The pathway stretched out in front of John. It was happening again. The road ahead was one he'd traveled many times, but every time was different. This time his shadow stretched out in front of him. Clouds swirled around a large dark tower looming in the distance. He knew no matter what choices were made from here on out that there would be no escaping the tower.

A shadow passed by him. He knew the power contained within the shadow. It was a glimpse into the thoughts and dreams of another Lavaliere. One touch and he would see what they saw, hopes and dreams and memories. All contained within a small shadow. All he needed was a glimpse at what the shadow conveyed and he'd be able to see the truth, enter into his friend's thoughts, and get a better understanding of how they felt. This one took on the form of a small creature with frosted fur and small eyes. John knelt down and reached out to pet the shadow, and when they made contact, the memories pulled him in.

The scene shifted, and before him, Jade stood at the edge of a cliff made of snow. John met her only recently when he'd arrived at Gem Haven. Jade's father, Pavlovian, had designed the place to take on the appearance of a hotel. It was a safe place for Lavalieres.

The extent of her control over ice and cold were still very much unknown to John. Her gem gave off a bright green glow, causing a blizzard to pick up. He fought against the howling wind. Knowing it wasn't real didn't make it any less difficult.

She turned and looked at him, an icy tear in her eye. "I don't want anybody's help."

John held out a hand, beckoning her away from the ledge. There was no time for her to come to him. He moved to pull her away, and she swayed. Her footing gave way, and she fell along with the avalanche.

"Jade!" John ran over to the edge and peered down into the abyss below, but all he could see was the squall.

The dream grabbed hold of him and pulled him away from the edge, back to the path. The tower was far darker, and taller, as though Jade's decision pulled him closer to the darkness.

A second shadow appeared, but just as he was about to reach out for it, Milo's hand clamped down on his arm. Milo was his link to everything, the whole reason he came to Gem Haven in the first place. John frowned, having expected warmth from the touch of his...*boyfriend*? Two thoughts came to him in rapid succession. The first was that he had nearly forgotten Milo lost his bond with his bloodstone. And the second was that he really didn't know what to think about their relationship.

A moment of clarity washed over John. He was asleep. None of this was real.

The shadows around him stopped moving, frozen

in time, and then they all turned on him at once, bombarding him with images, thoughts, and memories.

Something furry was in his hands. He looked down and saw a stuffed rat.

The dream manipulated Mark's orange and black striped body, shrinking him down into a tiny housecat version of his former tiger self. The small kitten's head turned as he pawed at the stuffed rat in John's hand. The sight was just silly enough to cause John to forget about his pain, and he let out a soft chuckle.

The shadows around John stopped moving, frozen in time, and turned on him, bombarding him with images, thoughts, and memories.

"I'm not weak." Mark whimpered.

"Follow the stars," an old woman said.

"Help me!" A young girl with auburn hair cried out. John reached for her, but she slipped away replaced by another nightmare.

"You can't stop me, I will rise again!" said a shrouded figure, his voice powerful and dark. *Igneous.* The figures sped toward the pillar.

John, trapped under the weight of the shadows, couldn't make any sense of the images speeding past.

"Wake up," Milo demanded.

John woke in a cold sweat, twisted in a pile of damp hotel bed sheets. Images flashed like distant memories already fading away.

The bed beside his own? Empty. This marked the third night in a row Milo sneaked off after John fell asleep. Igneous' attack had left a mark on each of them, especially Milo.

The full moon outside left a blue cast in his room for the past week. It wasn't real. What was?

He reached into the nightstand beside the bed and pulled out a small bound notebook. The book had no designated back or front. One side featured a bright landscape and was labeled: Day Dreams, but on the flipside was the polar opposite. A dark, yet peaceful labyrinth under a blanket of stars labeled: Night Dreams. The double-sided dream journal provided an outlet to dump those images and clear his head.

In the time it took to flip to a fresh page, the dream was already warping. The minor details grayed and blended together. Of those memories that hadn't faded, he jotted down the most important. Igneous was back. Three underlines, two exclamation points.

The flashes of images played out as a nightmare—warnings served on a silver platter.

He thumbed back to some of the first few pages. The very first entry, dated for the day after he'd bonded with his quartz. The journal, a gift from his mom for bonding, marked the beginning of his vivid nightmares, and the end to a normal sleep pattern.

He flipped back to the beginning, the very first nightmare. A short description written in jagged letters from a trembling hand.

The monster in the cloak is real. He breathes down the back of my neck while I sleep.

A click originating from the lock of the hotel door caused John a brief moment of panic, as if he'd been caught cheating on an exam. He shoved the sacred journal under his covers but was certain he was too slow. Milo walked in, surrounded by the halo of light coming from the hallway.

"You're up early," Milo said as he closed the door and shut them off from the rest of Gem Haven. The room shrouded in darkness.

"You're out late…" John countered. He pushed his nightmare aside. Milo fiddled with the lock, taking a moment before responding.

"I needed to go for a short walk."

Milo appeared to be constructing his response, picking and choosing his words carefully to keep the statement true. However, John wondered what Milo was keeping secret, while dodging John's ability to decipher truth from lies.

"I'm tired. Can we talk about it in the morning?" Milo yawned.

John nodded and Milo crashed on to the other bed. John realized he was playing a game of chicken when it came to expressing his emotions toward his roommate.

Those three little words.

John had been waiting a long time to hear them, but even he knew the timing had been premature.

In time.

"Wha…?" Milo mumbled.

John clamped his mouth shut. Had he said that out loud? He studied Milo for a few seconds and calmed down. Milo was talking in his sleep again.

As Milo turned, wrapping himself tighter in the blankets, John sighed. Milo would be embarrassed if he knew how cute he looked to John.

A cramp traveled up John's leg as he counted the seconds, not daring to move until he was sure Milo had fallen asleep. Only then did he feel comfortable enough to pull the notebook out from under the covers. Despite how tired he was, it would be impossible to fall back asleep.

Only John knew the truth behind his "chance"

encounter with Milo. Sometimes fate needed a little push. These were secrets he hadn't even shared with Milo. He opened to a particular page, the top corner bent in as a placeholder. An entry he'd reread dozens of times.

I left home without even saying goodbye.

If he hadn't, there was a good chance Milo wouldn't have made it to Gem Haven. He'd scribbled out a hasty note to his parents and left before the sun had a chance to peek over the horizon. The dream that woke him had left him numb. Igneous was going to stop at nothing to get what he wanted, more power. Igneous' schemes seemed foolproof, but there was one variable he hadn't accounted for, and that was John.

The power and focus of his dreams only grew stronger when the subject was Milo. Every decision, every possible path, played out for him in the shadows of his dreams. Knowing what was at stake made him feel both powerful and helpless at the same time.

There's this boy who keeps showing up in my dreams. He can't be much older than I am. And he's cute, but I don't want to get my hope up. He's probably not into guys, let alone guys like me. More importantly, I think the cloaked man is after him. If I don't help him, he's going to die. But if I do help him, I'll die.

John still had considered his actions. Only when he'd entered the airport did he realize the absurdity of his plan. What were the odds of encountering the guy of his dreams by running away from home and hopping some random flight? Slim to none.

He then spent some time searching the airport for him with no luck. He'd contemplated turning around and heading back home when a metallic taste filled his mouth. It was as if he'd licked a rusty hammer. When he looked up and saw a small Milo standing at the front of security, holding a hand out for the guard to inspect, he thought, "It's him, I still have a chance to warn him not to get on the plane." Then he'd spun on his heel, knocked into a sign, and spilled his piping hot tea down the front of his only shirt.

Milo turned out to be as kind as he was cute, offering to help pay for a replacement. Due to the course of events, it would have been impossible to keep Milo off the plane. The best he could hope was keep him safe until they arrived at Gem Haven.

"I'll make it up to you," John had said as the announcement for the flight came over the loud speaker.

He'd wondered, *What's next?* And an image filled his senses. *Auger in seat 5a.* He had to get there first. He'd taken off for the terminal.

He'd considered explaining everything to Milo who'd been with Lily and Mark. But he worried that either they wouldn't understand, or they would laugh it off. Either way, he hadn't had the time to waste on explanations.

"Excuse me, would you be willing to move so my wife can sit here?" the guy next to him had asked. Milo already had passed the seat, which meant another crisis averted.

John stood before he replied, "Certainly." He didn't take his eyes off of Milo. He felt the gears of fate turning, pushing the two of them closer. He forced his way through the crowded aisle. As he neared Milo, he noticed the bloodstone embedded in his hand.

Unfortunately, the hostess may have spied the gem

too. She'd been helping put luggage in an overhead compartment when John recognized her cufflinks, a diamond shaped design worn by augers. If she'd actually seen Milo's gemstone, he'd be in trouble.

John pushed forward, bumping into Milo just hard enough to send him to the floor. The commotion brought attention to Milo, causing him to become aware that people were looking in his direction and he hid his hand.

John had sighed, realizing for the first time that keeping Milo safe was going to be a lot more difficult than he expected.

****

Milo shifted in his sleep. John closed the notebook with a soft clap and hid his dream diary back in the drawer. The way he'd forced their first meeting felt almost like lying. Thinking about how much he'd concealed from the group made him feel sick to his stomach. But if not for him, Milo might not have survived.

The window screen buzzed. The moon jumped to a higher position in the night sky. John had lost count of how many times the program restarted since they'd been there. His hand hovered over the remote, contemplating powering down the screen. He knew the second he switched off that Milo would wake up and hound him to turn it back on.

Instead, he got out of bed and threw on a pair of pajama pants. Maybe a walk would help him clear his thoughts and worries. When he stepped out into the hallway, he had to shield his eyes from the sudden change in lighting.

In his haste, the door closed behind him, the lock

clicking into place. *Crap.* He felt his pocket for the key card, but knew he wouldn't find it there. He pictured it still sitting on the nightstand.

A steady bass beat pounded out a rhythm in what should have otherwise been a silent hallway. He followed the noise across the hall, pressing an ear up against Mark's door. The vibrations cut through to his core.

He backed up a step and knocked. No answer. He knocked harder. Still no answer. He pounded on the door. If that didn't get Mark's attention, nothing would.

The music stopped but John didn't hear any further movement within the room. Without warning, the door opened, and John's heart leapt to his throat.

"Fine, I'll turn it down." A tall half-human, half-tiger stared down at him with tired, golden eyes. Mark stretched, arching his back and baring his sharp teeth during a mighty yawn then focused. "Oh, hey John. Sorry, was the music too loud?"

"I didn't have a problem with the volume." John wondered how many complaints he'd received. "I kind of locked myself out of my room," he explained, scratching at the back of his head.

John tried not to stare, still not quite sure how he felt about Mark's new look. Any guy would kill for such a buff physique, but the head-to-toe fur made him appear more tiger than human.

Mark's gemstone was hidden deep in his chest fur. He was bonded with a tiger's eye, a stone known to shift and change depending on how one looked at it. Like the stone, tiger's eye bestowed the ability of shapeshifting.

Yet, Mark had the unique opportunity to choose

how others saw him. Of course, he would choose a form somewhere between human and animal, drawing as much attention to himself as possible.

"What's with the music?" John asked.

Mark sauntered across the room. His feline paws fell muted against the floor. He hopped up onto the bed, barely disturbing the mattress. Impressive. John fell on to the couch, springs squealing under his weight. If Mark's body was like a feather, his was a brick in comparison.

"I need the music loud. Otherwise I can't get any rest. These ears, they're great, I love them. But they pick up every little thing. It's like they have a mind of their own, they turn toward sound." Mark's tail wrapped around his leg. His fur-covered ears sat more toward the top of his head. Every so often one would twitch, picking up a sound John couldn't hear.

"Wouldn't loud music be a problem then?" John asked.

"Not really, the music is a constant single source of sound. It's just background noise at this point," he replied.

"Why not just change them back to human then?" John pointed out the most logical solution, but by the way Mark recoiled, he gathered making that suggestion was taboo.

"And risk looking like a freak? No thanks. This is comfortable to me, and anything different makes me toss and turn all night."

John found himself relaxing in Mark's company. One topic flowed into the next, and he learned a lot about Mark and Milo's pasts, and how the whole group had become friends. It was nice just listening, laughing, and not caring about anything for a change.

"Wait, wait. Let me try again. Two truths and one lie." Mark's fascination with his ability gave him a strange sense of pride.

"Okay, go ahead." John grinned.

"Okay. One, my mom thought I was going to be born a girl. Two, I failed first grade. Or three, my favorite fruit is pineapple." As Mark said the final statement, a sour taste bubbled up from the back of John's throat.

"Too easy, pineapple is the lie. Wait…you failed first grade?" The two of them laughed.

"Yeah, guess I refused to sit still long enough to learn anything." Mark leaned back against the head of the bed, grinning with pride.

"I can believe it," John replied.

"You're good, but I will get past your radar." Mark winked, holding firm to this belief.

"You know, most people just bend a lie until it becomes the truth." John grimaced at his own statement. Milo had been incorporating this tactic a lot lately.

"Nah, I want a bit of a challenge. One more try," said Mark.

John spent half the night on Mark's constant one more tries. He verified each batch of statements, much to the tiger boy's dismay, as the conversation continued well into the morning hours. It was hard to believe they'd only recently become friends.

Chapter Two

John hoped to catch up with Milo before dinner the next day, but the longer he paced the lobby waiting for him, the more he realized Milo wasn't going to show up. Mark and Lily kept attempting to ease his mind, but neither of them firmly believed Milo was going to join them. Even Lily's healing powers couldn't mend the wall Milo had put up between them.

John shuffled in place. Renovations to this common area had been made so effortlessly it made him uneasy. It was hard to believe Igneous, along with a group of Lavaliere-hating Augers, had successfully invaded their safe haven. He'd used Milo and the bloodstone bond they had in common to track down Gem Haven's hidden location. Waxed and polished floors, a sparkling new mahogany countertop, and plush seating covered up any signs of the previous battle damage from the days before.

He perked up, hopeful at every person entering the lobby, only to be let down when it turned out not to be Milo walking through the doors. To make matters worse, those who were coming through appeared to avoid their little group. Even among other Lavalieres, they had become the freaks of Gem Haven.

"He's not coming, is he?" John asked nobody in particular.

"Give him time. He's still recovering." Lily gave

his shoulder a small pat. He wished she could wave her hematite and return everyone to normal.

As small groups came and went, John caught a few of them staring and pointing at Mark, but they refused to say anything aloud. One guy stopped and stared a little too long. Mark snapped his teeth and laughed as he ran from the lobby.

"You're scaring the guests," Jade called out, entering through one of the side double doors. She made her way over to the group and gave them each a hug. John was relieved to see her up and about. Like Milo, she'd been a bit of a recluse the past couple of days.

John shivered as he embraced her cooler body. A small part of him still remembered how it felt as her ice dagger penetrated his chest during his first and only Gembreakers' match. Death may be temporary at Gem Haven, but it was impossible to cast away the memory.

"Sorry, he gave me the purrfect opportunity." Mark winked. His cat jokes were quickly growing old and Jade didn't look like she was in the mood.

"Hey, we were just about to get dinner, care to join us?" Lily extended an invitation to Jade.

"I don't know, I was supposed to meet with my father, but I can't seem to find him. Apparently he's too wrapped up in his experiments." Jade kept looking to the elevator, and John knew exactly how she felt.

"Riley suggested we try the Green Derby Diner, have you been there?" Lily asked. John had difficulty reading Jade's expression. Her apparent hesitation had John wondering if there may be something wrong with the place.

"We're leaving the hotel?" Jade appeared skeptical.

"Well, yeah. It's not like we can stay cooped up in here forever, right?" John asked. The hotel was beginning to feel more like a prison.

"No, but...I mean, we've managed to keep this place off the radar and I think some of us might draw a lot of attention." She motioned to Mark.

"I understand. I'm so good looking people are bound to notice." Mark grinned. John rolled his eyes. Mark's firm belief in his narcissistic statement astounded him. "It's not like we haven't already drawn the attention of a super villain...Igneous, and we handled him," Mark continued.

"Sure, but we could have food delivered here, or maybe you could try to look a little more normal?" Jade asked.

"This is normal for me, I'm sorry it doesn't meet your standards," Mark replied, the tone of his voice turning dark and serious.

"No, you're right. I'm sorry."

Jade faded slightly, and a sour taste flooded John's throat like bad acid reflux. He cringed, but kept his mouth shut. It wouldn't benefit anyone to wag a finger at Jade's fake apology.

A low rumble broke the awkward silence that followed. John realized the sound was coming from Mark's stomach.

"What? I can't control my hunger. It's been hours since lunch." Mark licked his lips. John didn't like the look in his friend's eye. To a tiger, just about anything could count as food.

John glanced at his watch and said, "Only three."

"See? Hours. I can't wait any longer. Milo will just have to fend for himself." Mark turned to Jade. "You don't have to join us if you don't want to." Mark offered her the opportunity to back out.

"I'll go. It has been too long since I've left Gem Haven. Besides, somebody has to make sure you guys don't get yourselves into trouble." Jade gave in.

John took one last hopeful glance at the elevator doors, as though he could will them to open up, as though he could somehow make Milo magically appear ready to join them on their quest for dinner. But the doors didn't open. Milo wasn't coming and John had to accept that.

As he made his way to the lobby entrance, he thought about the dream from the night before. Jade wasn't the only one standing on the edge of the cliff. He was too. This was his cliff, and maybe Jade had the right idea. He needed to take the leap into the unknown.

John took his first step back into the real world. He took a deep breath, and the sharp scent of pine flooded his senses. Everything out here felt crisper, stronger, and most importantly, real. There was a sense of honesty and truth in the world around him, things that had been lost inside the fantasy of Gem Haven.

Jade seemed hesitant to leave the safety of the building, stopping at the entrance as though the threshold was an invisible barrier keeping her inside. Lily took her hand and helped her out. As the door closed behind them, it shimmered under Swift's perception filter and disappeared, leaving them standing at the end of a small path in the forest.

As close as they all had grown over the past week, John continued to feel like the odd man out. He envied Jade's confidence. She and Lily picked up right where they left off. According to Milo, they used to go to the same school before Pavlovian moved his daughter to Gem Haven to keep her safe from Igneous.

"I just need to make sure I'm back in time for practice tonight. The Gembreakers' tournament is this weekend. Now that the ban is lifted, we need all the practice we can get," Jade said as she fiddled with her necklace.

"How's Chloe doing?" Lily asked.

John realized he hadn't thought about how the battle with Igneous had affected others outside their little group. He'd been so preoccupied with Milo he hadn't spent much time thinking about anyone else involved. Chloe's shadow had been dissipated by an auger, causing her to fall into a coma.

"No change," Jade replied, shaking her head. "Do you think her shadow is gone for good?" Lily asked.

"I don't know." Jade replied.

It seemed like the conversation was going to cut short there, but then Lily asked, "Did you find a replacement for the team?"

"Yeah, why, did you want to join us?" Jade asked, looking over at Lily.

"No! No. I'm okay, was just wondering." Lily's eyes widened, and she gave a small nervous chuckle.

As they made their way down the road, John wondered if anyone would even care if he never went back. If he just up and left after dinner, he could go on with his life. But he couldn't. Even just thinking about leaving Milo behind brought about a feeling of emptiness within him.

A truck sped up from behind, muffler rumbling as it careened up the long stretch of road.

"Vehicle approaching," John announced and the

group shimmied toward the curb.

The brakes squealed as the truck approached. It drew closer, and John could make out multiple dents and dings along the exterior. Tied to the front grill was a set of deer antlers, John couldn't know if they were real or fake.

"Filthy anthro." A buff looking guy in the passenger seat had his sunburned arm out the window. He took a swig from a brown bottle and then threw it out the window.

The bottle hit Mark and then fell, smashing on the side of the road. The truck sped off faster than John's heartbeat. His mind took a moment to catch up with the situation and convince himself it wasn't his imagination.

They all stopped, and John took a moment to remind himself to breath.

"Are you okay, Mark?" Lily pulled out her hematite.

"I'm fine, really, fine." He turned and picked up his pace.

John looked down at the smashed glass, shook his head, and raced to keep up. Jade muttered what sounded like *I knew it*.

Mark said nothing, but John saw his tiger ear twitch in her direction.

They continued on with little conversation, the air no longer lighthearted and fun. The encounter had put a serious damper on their adventure, but Mark seemed determined to follow through.

The first sign of civilization was not the diner they were looking for, but instead a small convenience store. John had half a mind just to give up on their walk, pick up a couple of microwave meals, and bring them back to Gem Haven

"Can you guys give me a moment? I just need to run in and grab something real quick." Jade announced and made a beeline for the door. John didn't think anything of it until he noticed the familiar truck parked sideways, taking up more than one space.

"I'll be right back, too." John ran to catch up. He had to stop her from doing something she'd regret. As he stepped inside, he felt the sudden drop in temperature, as if someone had turned the air conditioner on full blast. A thin sheet of ice coated the tiled floor, and John slid down an aisle where Jade had one of the guys pinned up against the frosted glass of a refrigerator. The frost was new.

"Might want to think about who you're pissing off next time." A flurry surrounded the guy's hand, solidifying and forming a thin layer of ice over his palm, effectively freezing him to the door. As he tried to pull away, the glass behind him creaked, threatening to shatter.

"This is what you call 'keeping a low profile'?" John surveyed the damage she'd caused in such a short period of time.

"He deserves it. Want anything?" Jade turned her back on the guy and made her way up to the front. She picked up a candy bar and handed it over to a terrified worker trembling behind the counter.

A spindled rack at the edge of an aisle captured John's attention. One item in particular called to him. A plush rat. It didn't just look like the one from his dream. There was no doubt in his mind this was the same one he'd envisioned. He picked up the toy and gave it a squeeze. The contents crinkled and felt stiffer than cotton.

"And this." John put the rat down on the counter.

"Catnip? Mark's going to flip shit. Good call." Jade reached for her pocket and the worker winced.

"Just take it miss, please, I don't want any trouble." The teen threw his hands up in surrender. Jade grunted at his remark, but threw a couple dollars down on the counter and scooped up the wares.

"This is catnip?" John asked quietly, and she nodded. He pocketed the plush mouse and followed Jade out the door.

"All good?" Mark asked as they approached. John fumbled for a response.

"Didn't you guys notice the jerks from earlier were here?" John pointed over to the truck, which looked funny. If he wasn't mistaken, it appeared to be sitting closer to the ground.

"Didn't notice a thing," Mark said while picking small flecks of rubber out from between his fingers. "We should get out of here"

"Agreed," Jade said, much to everyone's surprise.

John kept glancing back along the path to make sure they weren't being followed. Even though there hadn't been any sign of them for a good distance, he still didn't feel right about the way Mark and Jade had reacted.

Mark kept sniffing the air as they continued on their trek. John actively ignored him, feeling the weight of his prize heavy in his pocket.

"Does anybody smell that?" Mark finally asked. John kept his mouth shut. "I must be hungrier than I thought," Mark concluded.

As the sun lowered behind the trees, they made their way up to an older building with emerald green wood siding that showed the wear and tear of years gone by. Just above the door, a decorative star was built into the frame.

John's mouth watered as the smell of fresh baked breads carried them toward the diner.

"It will be fine," Mark said, even though his expression was one of concern. John could imagine how big of a moment and decision this was for him. This would be his first time showing off his new body in public, and hoping for acceptance. And after the incident with the truckers, it was no small feat to put faith in whomever they might run into next.

A momentary grip of panic spread through John, remembering how he felt when he first came out to his classmates back in middle school. He never expected the people he cared about most to hold such polarized views. Coming out helped show him who he could trust and who he needed to give up as a friend.

John braced himself for the worst. Rusted hinges creaked as the door swung open. A metal arm brushed against a small bell hanging just above the entry that rang out the announcement of their arrival.

An elderly woman appeared from around the corner carrying a stack of menus. A pair of thick glasses dangled from her neck by a rainbow band. Something about her seemed very familiar to him, but he just couldn't put his finger on where he'd seen her before. Her eyes fell on Mark, and she stopped, the menus dropping from her hands. She didn't need the glasses to see he wasn't entirely human.

"EARL," she screamed. So far, they were off to a

great first impression.

"It's okay," Mark said finishing with a low growl that did nothing to help his case. A much larger man burst through the kitchen doors, wielding a shotgun.

"What's wrong, May?" The grizzled old man also appeared to have eyesight issues, but not bad enough to keep him from seeing Mark. He took one look at the tiger, and his face went red.

"Wait. It's just a costume and makeup," Mark yelled, his image shimmering. John felt his quartz grow heavy with the weight of the lie. As risky as it was, he knew what he had to do.

John focused his voice through the stone and said, "He's lying, he's a Lavaliere, part man and part tiger. But he isn't here to hurt you. We just want dinner. So please, put the gun down." John's energy drained through the stone. He pushed the suggestion deep into the gun wielder's subconscious. The man placed the gun down on the counter, and John breathed a sigh of relief.

"Well of course not, but ya come bargin' in here, and ya gonna give someone a right scare."

"We're sorry, we didn't mean to," Lily said.

"I don't know what our girl is thinking sending another anthro here without forewarning." May bent over and picked up the menus, tucking them in the crook of her arm.

"What?" Jade asked. May shook her head and slammed a little black book down onto the counter next to the gun.

"Ain't like we've never seen your kind here before. We've lost more customers than we can count. If Ruby keeps sending you lot for a free meal, we're gonna be out of business." May led them down to a booth near the back. Before they could take a seat, she leaned over and lowered the blinds. A shadow fell over the table.

John shuffled into the seat, making room for Jade to sit down next to him. Mark sat across from him and Lily diagonally.

"Who's Ruby?" Jade asked when May was out of earshot.

John shrugged. He guessed she was their daughter based on how they talked about her.

"Who cares? Didn't you hear her say free meal?" Mark flipped open his menu.

John was stuck on another part of the conversation. When May said "your kind," he got the impression she wasn't referring to them as Lavalieres.

Chapter Three

John felt like he had been transported back in time. The diner had one long counter with stools from one end to the other. A row of booths lined the windows. On every booth there was a small replica jukebox, each one had tape over the coin slot and a sign that read: Out of order.

"Are we all ready, or do you need a couple of minutes?" May held a pen to the small scratchpad. John felt a little more at ease now that she seemed more interested in serving them than running them out of town with a pitchfork. They all nodded.

"Your tuna melt smelled amazing from the moment I walked in. I want two of them, a side of clam chowder…and a chocolate milkshake. Oh, and a side of fries." Mark rattled off item after item.

John shrank back behind his menu. May rolled her eyes, but tried to hide a chuckle, shorthand scribbling down each item.

"I'll just do a wedge salad and an ice water, thank you," Jade said, cutting Mark off short.

"I'll try the chicken noodle soup and a hot tea. Thanks." Lily smiled and helped gather the other menus. May turned to him.

His body still drained from the use of his power, John needed as much sustenance as he could get. But at the same time, he didn't want to impose the way Mark had. He settled on a burger and fries, and hoped it would arrive soon.

"You lot must be new at this. If you ever find yourselves in need of a meal, a room, or anything at all just follow the stars." May gave a small nod to John. She flipped the notepad closed as she walked away from the table.

"What do you think she means?" Jade asked.

John's ears were ringing. He'd heard those words before. They rattled around inside his head.

"She seems sweet. Reminds me of my mom," Lily said.

"Yeah, I guess." Jade pulled herself farther up in the seat. A silence fell over the table.

A television set hung down from the ceiling just above Mark. John glanced up just in time to see his picture flash across the screen. The camera panned in on a news anchor. He couldn't hear the story they were reporting, but he didn't need to. A large banner scrolled across the bottom declaring *Lavalieres Missing*.

His glass of water fell from his hands, clattering against the table. He grabbed for the cup, trying to keep it upright, but only managed to knock it away. The girls jumped from the table as water flowed down from the tablecloth and onto their seats.

"John," Jade yelled. She grabbed a few of the napkins to help keep the water contained. He kept nervously glancing over to the television, hoping the story would change before anybody noticed his picture plastered all over the screen.

"I'm sorry," he apologized to each of them.

The girls excused themselves to the bathroom while Mark ran napkins over his fur. As bad as he felt,

John couldn't help but laugh as the napkin fell apart, leaving scattered white specks dotting the orange and black.

"You've got to be kidding me." Mark huffed, picking out the pieces one at a time. John hadn't done it on purpose, but he'd managed to keep the attention off the news story long enough for it to change.

May came running out from the back with a washcloth to clean help clean up the table.

John dabbed at the couple of places he'd been splashed, nothing that wouldn't evaporate with time.

"I have a bit of bad news, our shake machine is out of order, is there anything else I can get you?" May finished wiping up the tablecloth and set down the drinks she had, all except Mark's.

"Fur real? Got any cub soda? Thank mew." Mark flashed her a big smile, and John cringed at each of his puns.

"Oh, you're just a house cat in a tiger's body, aren't you?" She laughed and gave him a playful tap on the shoulder before walking off.

"Can I tell you something?" Mark asked once May was out of earshot.

"Sure," John said, not really giving his request much thought.

"You can't tell anybody," Mark insisted, and John became a bit wary about what he as agreeing to.

"You know I'm not the best person to confide in, if I lie." John shook his head, realizing he was about to give away more information than was necessary.

"I know, but I have to tell someone." Mark's voice came across heavy with the weight of sincerity.

"What is it?" John couldn't help but feel a sense of

eager curiosity.

"I think I like Jade." Mark's eyes were staring off into the distance. John sat back in his seat, half expecting his powers to activate and expose Mark's lie. But they didn't.

"Never mind, it's not like she would ever be interested in some*thing* like me," Mark said. His eyes narrowed, and John turned to see what Mark was looking at. The girls were done cleaning themselves up and returning.

"Weird, Jade just came out of the wrong bathroom." Mark's change in conversation made clear to John he didn't want to continue talking about it.

Mark found a way to jump back into conversation with the girls as though the two of them had sat there in silence the entire time the girls were away. John on the other hand, withdrew with his new knowledge.

"Hey, you know what?" Mark said, "We're kind of like superheroes. We should come up with nicknames."

"Why?" Jade asked.

"Every great superhero has a nickname. Come on Icegirl, what's not to like about nicknames?"

"That's exactly what I dislike about nicknames, they're restrictive, they're demeaning, and they can be sexist. They cling to one or two qualities and pigeonhole them as a strict definition of a person." Jade stopped to take a breath, sipping from her ice water, her hand shaking as she lifted the glass.

"Sounds like someone is a little cold to the idea." Mark laughed at his own joke and Jade shot him an icy glare from across the table.

"Call me by my name, nothing else. If I hear you use the name Icegirl one more time, after I get through with you, you'll be wishing you had ice." Jade slammed her drink down on the table and went back to eating her salad. Mark threw his hands up in surrender.

"How can you be opposed to nicknames if you already have us calling you by the name of your gem?" John asked. Milo had told him her real name was Chloe, but she preferred the name Jade. From across the table, Lily shot him a warning glance, and he knew he'd said a little too much.

"There's a difference. Do you know how confusing it can be with two Chloe's on the same team? Can we please just drop it?" Jade was beginning to look uncomfortable. Her face drained of its color.

He'd accidentally touched a nerve.

"Hold on," Mark said.

"No, there's no reason for us to come up with nicknames." Jade's fingers gripped the water glass tighter. The condensation frosted, turning into glass beads along the surface of the cup.

"Shhh." Mark pressed a claw to his lips. His ears twitched, pointing toward the front of the diner. His golden eyes grew wide, whiskers twitching.

"Hey, John, you're on the news," Lily exclaimed, pointing to the television.

John didn't want to look. He couldn't bring himself to answer her. Admitting it was him on screen would only open up the conversation, which would lead to questions, ones he'd have trouble answering.

John dreaded seeing the story played back on a loop, but when he glanced at the television, the scene playing out told a very different story. A fuzzy black and white camera showed the time-lapsed interior of a convenience store. As bad as it was to see their escapades had already made the news, he actually felt somewhat relieved.

"They're here," Mark whispered. Just then the front door opened, the bell giving off a soft ring.

"Filthy beast. You owe me a new set of tires," one of the truckers yelled out.

"Sorry boys, but we're all closed up for the night," May called out to the newcomers as she brought over a tray with their meals.

"I'll take mine to go. I'll let Ruby know how great you were." Mark's form shimmered and a foul taste filled John's throat, momentarily distracting him.

John considered the possibility of implanting a suggestion on the truckers, but he still felt weak from the last one.

Earl walked out from the kitchen and cut off the trucker's path. "My wife said we're closed." Earl picked up the shotgun, making the trucker think twice about chasing after them.

Jade grabbed a pitcher of water off a nearby tray and poured it across the floor. She reached down and the thin layer of water turned into a thin layer of ice.

John slid out of the seat behind her and his foot slipped. His shoes slid out from beneath him, and he reached out for the nearest thing to hold onto. It happened to be the tray of food May brought out for them. The food went flying in all directions.

Mark pushed John aside, but wasn't fast enough to save his sandwiches from exploding on the floor. As John hit, the pain seared up through his bottom. The only good thing was he was already sitting on ice. Mark had to make the sacrifice, choosing to help John up instead of salvaging what he could of his meal.

They ran for the woods, utilizing the tree line for cover.

"I knew this wasn't a good idea," Jade repeated as though the confirmation would help change the decision they'd already made.

"Do you think they'll follow us? Maybe we should go in a bit deeper," Lily suggested.

John looked out through the trees, but without a good amount of light, he could barely make out the road, let alone see if the truckers had followed.

"Can't go back there again, no way they'd welcome us back," Mark lamented.

John had bigger worries though, constantly keeping an eye out to make sure they weren't being followed.

"Again with the running. I'm getting tired and hungry." Jade huffed, stopping to rub her calves.

"At least John should be used to it," Mark chided.

John shot him a *Why would you say that?* look.

"At least I don't constantly annoy the people I like," John said before he could stop himself.

"What do you mean?" Lily asked.

John pretended as if he didn't hear anything.

"You've been acting strange ever since we left the hotel. Are you okay, John?" Lily pressed and John knew he wouldn't be able to ignore her again.

"I guess." He regretted his answer and wished he could take back the last few seconds. He couldn't leave himself open to more questions or risk exposing his new knowledge.

"What do you mean?" Jade's questions may have been innocent enough, but they chipped away at his carefully constructed defensive barriers.

"Nothing," he screamed, hoping to put a halt to the

inquisition. The moment the lie crossed his lips, the world around him disappeared. *No,* he thought. *This can't be happening.*

He had been so careful not to slip up again. His lie set off the quartz, activating a dark side of his power. The area around him couldn't be described solely by a barren physical appearance. The best way to describe this mist-filled wasteland would be by the emotions it evoked. Emptiness. Loneliness. Depression. A place where nightmares are given life.

"Hello?" he called out, voice trembling. He'd been here before, when he hadn't yet known the drawback to his powers. A low growl came from behind him, and even though he knew it wouldn't be, he hoped to see Mark. Instead, he turned around and shook as he stared into the eyes of a large timber wolf. Even on all fours, she easily came up to his chest, her teeth bared with a bit of drool hanging from her jowl.

She lowered her head, but John knew it wasn't a sign of weakness. Her hind legs bent, prepared to tear him limb from limb at even the slightest movement. Her front paw tapped the floor, a motion he didn't recognize as lupine in nature.

With a guttural snarl, her broad frame dredged up the memory of the diner waitress' husband, Earl. Right then everything snapped into place. He knew the truth with every bit of his pounding heart. He swallowed and took a shaky breath.

"Ruby?" He called out to the wolf, raising his hand in a gesture of friendship. The wolf snarled and snapped at the air, but at the same time, there appeared to be a change in her attitude and body language. She backed up a step, ears perked.

She stood up on her hind paws, bones shifting, and breaking as they restructured themselves within her body. Her muzzle retracted, flattening to round out her facial structure. Her dark brown fur pulled back to reveal similar toned skin underneath, and her paws reshaped into hands and feet.

He couldn't believe the transformation taking place before him. Like seeing Mark become a tiger, but in reverse. A beauty rose out of the beast. The fur along her midsection did not recede throughout the transformation, instead shifting into an elegant faux fur robe wrapped majestically around her body.

The only part of her remaining distinctly wolf-like when the transformation had completed were her eyes. The golden orbs pierced through him, more feral than Mark's.

He'd been entranced by the transformation, but now as he got a good look at the girl standing in front of him, bells rang out in his head like an alarm.

"Ruby?" he called again and she nodded.

"Help...me..." She trembled, her voice shaky.

John wasn't sure how to react. Never before had another person joined him in his Dream Zone. He didn't get to reflect for long, the emptiness around them began to fill. First with a sweet smell, followed by thick rolling smoke. Through the smoke, an orange glow lit up the gray, pulsing.

A roar of air carried the sound of crackling embers toward them. The growing fire surrounded them on every side, giving no hope of escape. He turned, but the wolf girl had gone. Off in the distance, a howl echoed on the wind.

Chapter Four

John woke with a jolt, his shirt clinging tightly to his body, drenched in sweat. In those first few moments, he could still feel the flames lapping at him. He needed to write down everything.

He reached out instinctively for his journal, but his fingers wrapped around a clump of leaves and dirt instead.

"You did it. He's awake," said Jade.

Lily grunted and let the hematite fall from her hand, dangling at the end of the silver necklace. The clasp caught on her neck, causing the stone to swing back and forth as she knelt over him.

The putrid taste of battery acid bubbled at the back of his throat. He pulled himself into a sitting position and cracked as many stiff bones in his body as he could manage.

"How long was I out?" he asked.

"Only a couple of minutes," Lily replied.

John blinked, his eyes adjusting to the darkness of the forest. The others were there, but didn't say anything. "I saw her. She needs—"

"Help," a voice called out.

John jumped to his feet. The voice came from a bit deeper in the woods and sounded like it belonged to a girl.

"I see someone, there." Mark pointed, his eyesight

far better than the rest of theirs.

John squinted, but he didn't see her until she came out from behind a tree.

"Please," she said. "She was attacked and now she won't wake up. You have to help her." The girl had hair as dark as night. She was small in stature, but as she approached, twigs and branches snapped beneath her feet.

He recognized her as the dark haired girl from his dream.

"She's back there. She's hurt." The girl pointed to a small opening between two giant oaks.

John followed a path illuminated by the glow of the full moon. The others followed closely behind. He was right where he was supposed to be, at exactly the right time. He could feel it, and when he came upon a clearing, in the center was a metal cage. Inside the cage was a trapped wolf laying on the ground. Her chest rose and fell with the deep breath of a sleeping predator.

He walked up next to the cage and put his hand on a cold bar. Whether it was because he'd spoken to her in a dream, or maybe because he'd been hanging around tiger boy for so long, he had no fear of the trapped wolf.

"She won't hurt us. We have to help her," John insisted when the others caught up.

The girl who warned them was gone. They had to get her out of the cage, but a padlock on the door prevented them from rescuing Ruby.

John picked up a fallen branch and swung it at the lock. The lock moved under the force, but it didn't break. He moved to swing again, and Jade stopped him.

"Hold on." Jade grabbed the padlock and closed

her eyes. The metal of the lock lightened as her power lowered its temperature, but otherwise there wasn't much change in appearance. "Try now."

"I got this." Mark wrapped a paw around the padlock and pulled. With a snap, the lock broke off, and the door opened.

John held his breath as Lily knelt next to Ruby. She took hold of her hematite and put her other hand on the wolf's chest. She looked up and shook her head.

"It's no use." She sighed and stood up.

"You were able to wake John, right?" Jade asked.

"It's not a healable injury. Him waking up was a coincidence. If this is Ruby, we should take her back to her parents," Lily suggested.

"Not in this condition. We have to get her back to the hotel," Mark insisted.

"None of you are going anywhere. You'll pay for what you did to me and my truck." The guys from earlier had caught up. They blocked the path back. One of them now carried a shotgun.

John's pulse pounded, he hadn't seen this in any of his nightmares.

Before anybody could react, he pointed the gun at Mark and pulled the trigger. John jumped at the sound of the shot ringing through the trees. Mark dropped to the ground.

"No," Lily screamed and fell to his side. The guy already had the shotgun reloaded and raised it toward Jade. She was the only one left who could stop them. John jumped in front of his friend as the second shot rang out.

John knew he'd been struck. The hot sting of the bullet grazed his arm before making the sound of a clink just behind him. As much as his arm hurt from the blow, the more important issue to him was whether or not he'd been able to protect Jade.

"John," Jade yelled from behind a sheet of ice. The noise he'd heard was the bullet being stopped by the thick shield in front of her. Once again, he'd messed things up by trying to be helpful.

Jade let the shield and the bullet drop, and retaliated by throwing an ice dagger in their attackers' direction.

The world began to tilt as John looked down at his wound. His shirt had a tear where the bullet penetrated, and the material was beginning to stain red.

"Guys, I think you should know I'm not all that good with blood." The last thing John saw before he collapsed was Jade chasing after the guys, her face filled with a passionate rage.

****

John couldn't have been happier to see the familiar chandelier hanging from the ceiling of the lobby. He could still feel the pain in his arm but feared looking at the wound. When he did, he saw it had healed, likely by Lily while he was passed out.

"Careful there, how are you feeling?" The tiger leaned over him with a big goofy grin plastered on his face. John pushed his friend away and sat up.

"Where are the others?" he asked while attempting to stand up. The rush of standing up too fast made him woozy. He reached out and placed a hand on Mark's arm to keep from falling over.

"Lily was worn out and went to sleep for the night. Jade went to her practice, and Ruby was taken by Pavlovian." Mark took his arm and helped keep John steady.

"Hey guys, getting a bit close there, don't you think?" Riley had just come through the double doors leading from the regeneration wing of the hotel.

John was a bit slow in understanding what he meant but caught up when Mark brushed him off.

"Heard you guys saved a girl earlier. It's awful how often this has been happening, lately." Riley continued while shaking his head.

"Yeah, she—"

"Oh, I almost forgot that Milo left this for you. I guess you might have forgotten it this morning? Sorry, I can't stay and chat. Gotta get back. They can't start without their leader." Riley handed John his room key and darted off toward the Gembreakers' court.

Milo…he hadn't seen him at all since the previous night. It hit him harder than the bullet. How could Milo not even take the time to check on him and return the key card himself?

"Guess we should head back to the rooms." John tried to mask the sadness in his voice.

Mark led them into the elevator, the cold metal doors cutting them from the front lobby and opening only a moment later to empty out into a false hallway leading toward their designated rooms. The physics of Pavlovian's pocket dimensions made less sense than a child's fairytales.

They had been warned not to try to apply sense or logic to Gem Haven, but John couldn't help wondering how it could be possible for them to be in one location one second and then instantly teleport to another within the building.

He actively ignored the order. He had to call into

question whether or not any of this hotel existed in a physical space. Perhaps the entire place was a construct of Pavlovian's mind. Were they all walking around inside of Pavlovian's thoughts? What would that mean for those willingly stepping inside such a metaphysical place and how could Pavlovian enter?

He found himself subconsciously heading toward his own room. If he could make it back to the diary, he could write down his thoughts and experiences of the day...try to make it all make sense.

"Can we talk?" Mark looked as though he needed to get a few things off his chest.

"Oh, uh...okay." He abandoned the promise of sanctuary within his room to follow Mark to his. Mark closed the door behind them, trapping John.

"I wanted to..." He stalled as though reconsidering. "Can I asked why you ran away? Did your parents not accept you?"

John was completely taken aback by the questions.

"No, nothing like that. My parents are amazing. They accept me being into guys." His voice cracked as he spoke about them. "I didn't have any brothers or sisters, so they spoiled me a lot. I got to try all sorts of hobbies growing up. If I didn't like one of them, they wouldn't make a fuss about it." He went on, hoping if he just kept talking about them, Mark might open up about his own feelings.

"I don't get it then. What are you hiding from us?" Mark's choice of words was unfortunate.

"Why would you think I'm hiding something?" John asked, although he was certain his facial expression must have betrayed him.

"I can smell it. What aren't you telling us?"

Anything other than the truth about his dreams and what brought him to Gem Haven might feel too much like a lie, resulting in his quartz backfiring.

"I had to stop Igneous," he replied.

Mark gave him an offhanded look of slight disbelief.

"Go on…" Mark said.

John sighed and looked away. Moment of truth time. As he explained the disjointed images he began receiving after bonding with the quartz, he tried to get a sense of Mark's reaction. The tiger remained stoic, listening but not reacting. John stopped himself before he could bring up the most recent dream.

"Wait, you're saying you saw Ruby in one of these…visions?"

John nodded, and after what felt like a long period of silence, Mark asked, "Do you think we could help her?"

"I'm not sure," John admitted. "Why, do you like her? I thought you had a crush on Jade." He goaded, trying to get Mark on a different topic.

"What? No. I was just concerned," Mark offered. Once again John's quartz activated, and his power caught Mark in the lie.

"Earlier all you could think about was getting to dinner. You've got to come up with a better lie than that."

"Just seeing if you were paying attention." Mark's body shimmered, the fur beginning to grow transparent. John blinked, wondering if it was just his imagination.

"I'm sorry." Mark appeared before him once more and John jumped back in fright, nearly falling off the couch in the process. Nobody had ever lied to him consecutively before.

"I think we're both tired. I should head back to my room now." John gathered himself together, still a bit shaky and pulled out his key card.

"You're joking, right?" Mark asked. "We've asked ourselves what one day can possibly change in the past, and the answer was always far too much. We're going to find Ruby tonight." Mark winked.

John wasn't sure if he should be comforted by the fact Mark seemed to be telling the truth, or worried his friend might have jumped off the deep end.

"How are we supposed to do that? Do you happen to know where the infirmary is in this upside down carnival funhouse?" John pointed out the major flaw to Mark's plans.

"Nope, but I'm pretty sure I know someone who does."

****

John found himself looking out across a familiar courtyard. On the field were six pillars and a small group of Lavalieres.

Jade and her team were out on the field facing off against Riley's newest band of uncoordinated recruits. The match was in no way a fair one, with Sophia leading their team toward a decisive victory.

There was something morbidly exciting about Gembreakers. Jade flung a few icicles in the direction of the defenders from the opposing team. The girl who rolled off her pillar and face planted on the ground below was Nina, the girl who checked them into Gem Haven when they first arrived.

Jade jumped onto Nina's pillar, tagging it for the point. The stone lit up from inside. Jade wasn't finished though, she used the momentum from her leap to push herself into the central defense pillar, scaring the defender off and securing a second point. Finally, she ran to the edge and leapt onto Riley's. As he fell to the ground, Jade singlehandedly took the win for her team.

"Jade," Mark yelled. He motioned to get her attention, but she was either actively ignoring him or remained oblivious. Instead, she made her way over to one of her teammates who was sitting on the ground rubbing her shoulder. Jade placed a hand on her teammate's arm and small ice crystals formed where she made contact with the uniform.

"I think she's giving us the cold shoulder." For once Mark's pun seemed purely coincidental.

"I'm pretty sure she's giving her friend a cold shoulder." John picked up on the opportunity, but immediately felt a shame in grabbing such low hanging fruit.

"Nice, you might be worth keeping around after all." Mark smiled and winked.

"Hey, Icegirl." Mark knew just what would get her attention. Not that it was the kind of attention he needed. This time the nickname grabbed her attention. She turned, glaring, and shot an ice dagger in his direction. John was quick enough to push him out of the way, and it smashed against the wall behind them, raining small shards down on the ground.

"I told you to never call me that. What do you want? And be careful, you're walking on thin ice." A cold front swept through with her arrival. John saw the gears turning as Mark's whiskers twitched. John shook his head and mouthed "no," hoping Mark would take the hint and let the opening drop.

"Chill out," he replied and chuckled. John sighed. This exchange was getting them nowhere.

"Ugh," Jade yelled, her lips turned blue, and small ice crystals formed on her eyelashes. If he didn't mitigate this fast, she looked ready to turn Mark into a tiger ice statue.

"We need your help." John stepped between the two of them. "You've been here longer than anybody. Can you take us to Ruby?"

"The infirmary? Is it urgent? We only just started our fifth practice." She looked over at Mark.

"Can you take us there?" John asked again, but Jade seemed hesitant.

"Since you're the one asking and not the pretty kitty over here, yeah, I can take you there."

"Aww, you think I'm pretty." Mark arched his back with pride while Jade rolled her eyes.

"We'll pick back up tomorrow," she called out to her teammates.

Chapter Five

John trailed behind the others entering the elevator. There were no buttons in this elevator. Instead, a small card scanner waited eagerly for one of them to hold up a room key.

Jade pulled out a black key card, very different from the keys given to them when they were assigned rooms in Gem Haven. He'd seen and used one of these special cards in the past. Pavlovian had given it to them after they defeated Igneous.

"Invalid access key." The computerized voice came from invisible speakers.

"Useless." Jade huffed and threw the card on the ground.

"How exactly do these elevators work?" John asked as the doors closed behind them. The tiny box felt even more claustrophobic than the windowless lobby from where they'd entered.

"Memory," Jade replied as she pushed on a portion of the wall next to the doors. With a click, a small panel door opened up to reveal a hidden console.

"Like thinking about where you want to go?" John asked. He peeked over her shoulder to get a better look at what she was typing.

"Does everything have to be fantasy with you? Computer memory. It accesses the location like a file on a server and opens it up to you. The key cards are like a shortcut on a desktop, they take you right where you want to go."

"And if you don't have the right card?" John flashed a glance at the discarded key on the floor.

"Have you ever gone searching for a file on your computer after you've forgotten where it is? That's basically what I'm doing, except without any search functionality." Jade's fingers continued to fly along like butterflies fluttering on the keys. Screens opened and shut. She stopped when a screen opened displaying the words "Medical Mezzanine."

"I found it. Odd. Someone password protected the floor." Jade pulled away from the keyboard.

"The medical wing is password protected?" Mark asked.

Jade didn't say a word. Instead, she returned to the keyboard and entered a string into the prompt. A red light flashed within the room and a loud buzzer pierced their ears. Jade stepped back, her face scrunched up in disgust. John put his fingers in his ears, but could still hear the alarm.

"I think you made a mistake," Mark yelled.

"This makes no sense. The encryption should be easy to crack...unless the hash changed recently." She stepped back up to the keyboard, a distinct change in the way she worked the keys. Before she was light-fingered and fast, now her strokes were clunky and slow. A message repeated itself on the monitor: "Please enter passcode." She entered a short string of random characters only to have a second message display after, "Incorrect passcode" followed by a countdown indicating how many chances remained.

"What happens when the countdown hits zero?"

John asked, trying to keep his voice above the alarm. Jade hit enter and the screen flashed with another attempt gone and no change in status.

"Let's not find out." She seemed uncertain but focused. John didn't like the implication. Would they be locked out of the system? He didn't want to be trapped. The walls began to press in on him. He knew the amount of space in the elevator hadn't changed, but it felt like this box was getting smaller. Another couple of attempts later and Jade slammed her fist into the wall. She had only one more chance.

Jade entered a masked input into the system and hesitated, finger hovering over the enter key. She shook her head, deleted the entry, and typed in something different. His confidence drained when he saw her close her eyes. She entered the passcode.

The alarms died out and the flashing red light shut off, leaving only the dim yellow ceiling lights remaining. John breathed a heavy sigh of relief. An elevator bell rang once and the doors slid open, revealing a darkened hallway beyond.

John shared a worried look with Mark. They'd been down this hallway before, led here by the special key card given to them by Pavlovian after the battle with Igneous. John shivered, but his trembling had little to do with the reduced temperature. He never thought he would come back here.

"Are you sure you have the right location for the medical wing?" Mark asked. Both of them stalled inside the elevator as Jade exited. Flashes of John's recent dreams flared up in full force, images of the Diadem danced across his vision. He gulped. The Diadem was a powerful tool used by Igneous in his attempt to infiltrate Gem Haven. The wearer had access to any powers corresponding to the inlaid gems without needing to have a bond to them.

"Yeah, at the end of the hall." Jade pointed down the long stretch of corridor while holding the elevator door open. "Are you coming?"

They stepped out into the hallway. A light above them flickered. This part of the building looked like it had been neglected for years, which explained why it could only be accessed by a select few. The elevator doors closed behind them. John's fingers trembled involuntarily and his feet tried to drag behind, not wanting to take him farther down the rabbit hole. But he needed to find Ruby. He needed to make sense out of what he'd seen in his dreams.

This uninviting part of Gem Haven resembled a basement more than a hallway of a hotel. Pavlovian clearly didn't want anybody randomly roaming down here.

Rooms with decaying doors gathered dust and looked like they hadn't been touched in ages. Though the room numbers had been removed, the outline remained visible, the difference obvious in the aged wood.

As with any other basement, he thought this area was used specifically for storage and losing things you no longer wanted. Why would a medical room be located so deep down a passageway like that?

He dragged his feet as they passed a specific room. This was the farthest he had traveled down this hallway. The room number etched into the door was framed by char marks that read "025". He knew the secret contained within was more powerful and problematic than any. It scared him. Pavlovian had made the decision to hide the Diadem rather than destroy it.

He pictured the Diadem in his hands, the new bloodstone set inside one of the previously empty loops of metal, just after it had been ripped from Milo's grasp. The smell of ash floating in the air had signaled its activation, much like it had every time Milo used the power.

"John?" Jade called out, and he realized he'd stopped moving forward. He blinked and cleared his throat.

"Sorry." His dry mouth made it difficult to speak. His muscles seemed almost locked in place, but he managed to pick up his foot and begin down the hall once more.

"Down there on the right," Jade whispered. Behind them, the elevator bell rang and gears clicked as the doors began to slide open.

"It's my father. Hide," Jade hissed and darted toward room 025.

"No," John and Mark screamed at the same time, pulling her across the hall. He hoped the extra time it took to course correct wasn't enough to give them away. The door slammed shut behind them, and John winced.

"He must have heard the alarm." Mark kept his voice low.

John backed deeper into the dark room. The sole source of light came from the glow of his watch. His foot caught on something hard, and he reached out with his hand to steady himself, catching and grasping the arm of something cold and hard.

John turned and shrieked, the green glow from his

watch reflected off the cool silver surface in front of him. John quivered, caught in the figure's menacing glare. The sunken cheeks and sickly dead look on the being's face, told John exactly whom he'd mistakenly bumped into.

"What's wrong?" Jade flipped a light switch, making the situation much worse.

"Igneous!" John fell back over his own feet, landing with a thud on the hard floor. His heart pounded in his eardrums as he scrambled to pull himself farther away.

Plink. An icicle whizzed past him and shattered against the statue's stone chest. John took a moment to mentally process what he was seeing. Standing in front of him, frozen in place, stood a solid stone statue replica of Igneous with his arm outstretched, lips locked in a snarl.

His panicked breath slowed when he realized the thing wasn't real and wasn't about to kill him. With Mark's help, he pulled himself up off the floor and slowly made his way to the inanimate villain. More statues filled the rest of the room, each with their own shocked or outraged expressions.

"What is this...?" Mark poked at the statue and jumped back as though he expected retaliation.

"This is Riley's doing," Jade replied. There had to be at least a dozen other statues. Each with their own intricate details giving them an eerie, realistic quality.

"What are you guys doing down here?" Riley's unexpected voice coming from behind John caused him to jump. Riley stepped into the room and said, "You're not supposed to be here."

"We came to find Ruby." John offered his excuse,

knowing full well that it didn't explain why they had wandered into such a strange room in the middle of the night.

"Don't worry about her. She'll be out of here by tomorrow. Go back to bed and let us handle it." Riley turned, as though he were about to leave.

"They're real." Mark let out a slow sigh as he navigated between statues, studying each one. Riley's presence barely seemed to faze him.

"Yeah, they are real and dangerous, that's why we keep them in stasis," Riley said.

"So they're still alive?" Jade asked, standing in front of a statue that didn't seem particularly threatening.

The statue was a woman of a much larger build with a serene look on her face. She stood in complete contrast to the others in the room. Her eyes were closed, and John could imagine her being at peace with her condition. An elegant stone dress flowed over her form. Her hands, held together in the front, gave her an air of royalty.

Something about this woman made him sad. He wondered what her voice would have sounded like if she could have spoken. Would it have been soft and caring? In his gut, he felt she didn't deserve this. He wanted to throw his arms around the statue and wrap her in a hug, but that would be silly.

"Everyone in this room posed a threat to our existence in one way or another. They were turned to stone in order to make our lives safer." Riley's distinct lack of compassion came as a sobering reality check. John tried to imagine what these people could have possibly done to deserve such an eternal punishment.

"Turn her back," Jade demanded.

"Nobody is here by accident. The last person to be stoned was Igneous, and you saw firsthand the kind of threat he posed." Riley's insight left John with a chill. The way he spoke about the statues, made it sound like they were in the presence of death row inmates. This was a prison. No, more like a dungeon.

"I don't have time for this." Riley turned and left the room.

"Mom…" Jade choked up, a tear rolling down her cheek.

John's heart sank as he realized the connection between her and this woman. Even Mark stood silent as she broke down in front of them.

"She was a kindhearted woman who would never hurt a fly. What could she have possibly done to deserve this?" Jade asked, but Riley was already gone, and Jade looked as if she had been slapped.

She gave the statue a hug. It no longer seemed silly. Jade turned and threw her arms around him. The cold embrace was difficult to maintain, but he held on as long as she needed him to.

"I'll cope." She pulled away, sniffing as she wiped away a tear from her eye.

"Are you sure?" Mark asked.

"Yes." She nodded. "Only Riley can bring her back. Let's go." She steadied herself.

John was at a loss for words. He wanted to help her, but wasn't sure if she was ready to accept help

"We're here for you." Mark set aside the puns and jibes to assure her they'd support her.

He paced the room, sharpening his claws with his teeth. He stopped in front of the statue of Igneous, raised his paw, and slashed across the stone face. The connection of claw against stone created a spark, and sounded like a key scraping across a car's frame, but didn't cause nearly as much damage.

"We need to get to Ruby," said Mark. "I get the feeling Riley may have been lying."

"Not possible, I would have known immediately," John replied, feeling a bit defensive about his abilities being called into question. Compared to his friends, his powers weren't the most useful of the bunch, and now Mark was accusing the one he did have of not working.

"Yeah, I know how your power works. I don't know…I picked up a very powerful scent coming from him. Like he was nervous or scared or something." Mark sniffed the air around them. "If you don't believe me, you just gave off a powerful scent. I'd guess anger. Look me in the eyes and tell me I'm wrong," Mark challenged.

"Okay, I believe you," John said.

"He knows more than he's letting on. Let's go find out what he's hiding." Mark pushed open the door to the room and let himself out.

Chapter Six

At the end of the hallway, they traded the dark, dingy corridor for the sterility of a brightly lit infirmary.

John gaped at the sight before him, a dozen or so cots lined the walls on either side, but what shocked him the most was seeing how many of them were occupied.

A few had their privacy curtains drawn, but there didn't appear to be a need. The unconscious patients were each hooked up to a machine. A steady rhythmic beat beeped in conjunction with a spike in the line being graphed.

John noticed two things about the heart monitors. The first was the rate, which seemed far too slow for a resting pattern. The second was how each machine's beeps were in unison.

John stood beside the nearest bed and looked over the setup. Diodes ran from the unconscious Lavaliere's shaved head up to a monitor hanging off to the side of the bed. A bright image displayed on the monitor comprised of spots of red, blue, green, and yellow. It looked a lot like a heat map he'd seen at a museum once. As he watched, the colors shifted in mesmerizing patterns.

"Neuroimaging. They're mapping brain patterns," Jade mused as she reached out and opened one of the patient's eyelids. Their pupils were no bigger than a pinpoint and completely unresponsive.

The Lavaliere's necklace hung from a hook in the wall behind the bed. Inside the setting was a beautifully cut sparkling diamond.

"They're all *precious gems...*" Jade announced from the foot of another bed. John looked over to see her hold up a ruby. Down the line, he could see sapphires and emeralds adorned other necklaces, each stone rare enough that Lavaliere bonds with them were practically unheard of.

A clatter came from the far side of the room where the privacy curtain had been drawn. If he had to guess, that's where they were going to find Riley.

Mark was the first one across the room, skidding to a halt just outside the partition.

"What exactly is your deal?" he asked and pulled Riley out from behind the curtain.

Then John caught up to the two of them and saw what snagged Mark's attention. There she was, like all the others, tethered to the hospital bed, eyes glazed over with a small beep from the monitor being the only indication of life. A few of the wire leads dangled off the side of the bed, the beeping heart monitor switched over to a constant hum as the green line flattened.

"You killed her!" Jade choked on her words.

"No, I removed her from the heart monitor. She's not supposed to be here. She's...my sister." Riley turned away from them, taking her hand in his. John noticed a faded scar on his forearm.

"What? You've never mentioned having a sister." Jade's features softened.

"I haven't seen Ruby since..." he said and hid his arm from view and shook his head. "Never mind, it doesn't matter."

"I saw her earlier, kind of," John mumbled and tripped over his words. He explained how she had come to him to ask him for his help, and how he'd seen her change.

"Nobody has come out of this coma, yet. If it's anything like the others, she won't wake up any time soon. We have to get her out of here." Riley ripped at the wires connecting his sister to the machine. The brain image froze on the screen.

"Help me get her out of here," Riley shouted as he dropped to the floor, fiddling with the cot's wheels. John didn't even hesitate. He jumped into motion and began helping Riley release the locks.

"What are you doing?" Jade asked, a mortified look on her face.

John felt the snap of the lock coming undone and moved to get the next one, but Mark had beaten him there. He'd already jumped in and completed the task. The three of them each took a side and helped maneuver the cot out into the middle of the hall and up the aisle toward the front of the room.

"Pavlovian won't listen to me. She can't be here if she wakes up," explained Riley as they wheeled her toward the door. "The walls aggravate her. They bring out the wolf instincts." He didn't go into too much detail, but John saw Riley scratch at the spot on his arm where he'd seen the scars.

"I get that entirely," Mark said, his ears twitching as they picked up on various sounds throughout the room.

"Wait...I hear him coming." Mark's ears now pointed straight toward the door to the room.

There was no doubt in John's mind they were going to be caught. They had just enough time to jump behind a curtain before the door burst open. He held his breath as two pairs of shoes tapped along the floor. One pair distinctly belonged to Pavlovian, but John couldn't see the second set from under the curtain.

"He's detailed every premonition in a dream journal." Milo stopped in front of the track partition where they were hiding.

John's muscles tensed and his knees threatened to buckle. Milo knew about his journal. He'd read everything. Not only the dreams but all of John's innermost thoughts and feelings as well. John's breath caught in his throat. He wanted to reach out and slap Milo for betraying his privacy, but doing so would expose them.

"He's not ready. We need to know how Felicia's manipulating the nightmares. Check on Ruby while I get set up for inducing lucidity." Pavlovian turned on his heel and moved away from their hiding place.

Milo followed. "According to his journal, Igneous could rise any day now."

"The two are very likely related in some way." Pavlovian slid a curtain aside, causing John's heart to leap into his throat until he convinced himself it wasn't theirs.

"Ruby's gone." Milo's voice echoed throughout the room, followed by the bang of something heavy crashing to the floor.

John's held breath escaped his lungs. What was Milo doing here? He stared through the curtain, and even though it blocked his view, he imagined he was looking directly at his love, casting unspoken accusations.

"She couldn't have gone far," Pavlovian's response seemed out of place. It almost sounded like they were expecting her to remain in a coma.

"It's not like she could get up and walk out of here on her own. And the bed is gone." The frustration in Milo's voice fueled the fires of betrayal by someone he so deeply cared for.

A tug on his shirt sleeve nearly caused him to jump out of his skin. Riley motioned with his hand, a sign of urgency understood by the group as "let's go while we still can." The resulting silent conversation was simple enough for John to follow.

Jade indicated "no" with a simple headshake.

Holding a single hand up, Riley's eyes narrowed, and his forehead scrunched questioning her.

John knew what she was thinking...*We'll get caught. They'll see and hear us as we try to leave*...because it was exactly what he was thinking. Jade attempted to convey all that with her multiple hand gestured charades. She then pointed to her shoes.

With an exaggerated eye roll before bending over and sliding his off, Riley pointed to his bare feet.

Good idea, John thought and nodded with a smile as he leaned over to untie his own.

Meanwhile Mark, who wasn't wearing any shoes, slung the wolf over his shoulder. His animalistic build gave him the strength to carry her with ease.

John hesitated, shoes in hand, listening for the smallest hint of a reason why Milo would have any interest in Ruby. Mark mouthed the word "now," and John knew he wouldn't get his answers. They dashed across the floor, hoping the machines would be loud enough to drown out the soft patter of their feet.

Riley tried to open the door quietly, but a long creak emanated, alerting the others to their presence.

"There. Stop," Milo yelled and began to make chase.

John was torn, part of him wanted to stop and let Milo catch up to them, but another part made him feel a sense of duty to Ruby and keeping her safe from whatever it was they had planned.

They ran as fast as they could back to the elevator, the last thing they saw was Milo and Pavlovian running toward them as the doors closed.

"Well that could have gone better. How do you suggest we get her out of here?" Mark and the others turned to Riley for the plan.

"We need to get her outside. Go to the lobby." Riley held up a key card but Jade stopped him before it could be scanned.

"I don't think that's a good idea. Gem Haven is the safest place for her," Jade said.

"You're just like your father. She needs to be outside," Riley argued.

"Wherever we are going, we should go now." John sank into the back corner, the cool metal walls pressing in on him from either side.

"I have an idea." Jade opened up the console and began typing away at the keyboard.

"It's a place I know better than anyone in Gem Haven. My dad made it for me when he first created the hotel. Back then, all I wanted to do was play hide and seek." Her face lit up under the warm rays of sunlight as the doors slid open to reveal a tranquil garden of flowers.

Endless blue sky stretched out in every direction. John made his way out into the field and turned to see the out of place elevator shaft standing alone as the sole piece of machinery among nature. Ivy crawled up the sides, giving it a dystopian aura and a sense no one had ventured here in quite some time.

"We're outside the hotel?" Riley asked.

"No, if we were it would be night. This isn't real." Even though he was standing perfectly still, a wave of dizziness washed over him and made John feel like he was falling. Like the courtyard, this was just another trick of Pavlovian's. Jade nodded an affirmation.

Turning away from the only connection currently tethering them to the hotel, he took a deep breath, but his lungs could tell this place still hung heavy with fraudulent air. They weren't actually outside. The false serenity proved to be another trick of the pocket dimension Pavlovian had created.

"Where are we? I've never seen this room before." Riley's ease of calling it a room only further conveyed his readiness to accept they were still trapped.

Mark carried Ruby over to a hedge archway and propped her up against the thicket, her body outlined by the small violet flowers blooming throughout. She looked peaceful and serene, but John knew the truth, she was trapped just as much as they were, if not more. A hedged wall drew up around the perimeter from the archway, creating a barrier more than two stories tall.

"It's the labyrinth. We can hide in here for now and regroup, give them some time to give up looking for us." Jade tapped her fingers to her thumb, her eyes squinting as they glazed over momentarily. She repeatedly mumbled two distinct words, left and right, as she mentally mapped out the design of the maze.

"Ready? Follow me." Jade breached the entrance of the maze and took off at a run. Her hand barely grazed the sides of the walls, and they all took an endless number of twists and turns, heading toward what John assumed was the center of the maze. Just as he was beginning to lose his breath, she stopped.

They had come to a section unlike any they'd passed before. Where most of the maze had been made of straight lines and sharp corners, this one stood out as the wall curved in a small outward arc. Another entryway marked by blue and yellow flowers led them inside a small sanctuary surrounded by a semicircular arc of hedging. In the center, a fountain made up of three separate stone statues stood tall.

The first statue resembled a young girl with a crown of thorns resting on the top of her head. Her face slightly upturned as she gazed over the second, a granite wolf that stood just over half her height.

The wolf's front paw hovered in mid stride, nose turned outward, giving a sense of protection to the fragile girl. She was his ward, and he would not allow any harm to come to her.

The third statue was the strangest of the set. It had the physique and build of a young boy, but the snarled face and sunken eyes told a different story. His hand, outstretched, reached for the girl with a bony finger. A pair of bat-like wings protruded from his back. But his appearance alone wasn't what spooked John. Somehow, the statue appeared to be floating above the others, as though the stone were lighter than air.

The optical illusion had required careful molding of the stone, shaped in such a way as to remain connected, ever so slightly, to the other fixtures. Knowing the engineering didn't make the statue any less creepy.

"What now?" Mark carefully laid Ruby down across the edge of the fountain, and took a seat next to her. He'd found just the right position to make it look like the imp wanted to eat him for breakfast. John shook his head, opting instead to sit cross-legged on the ground.

"Now we come up with a plan." Riley picked up a flat rock and skipped it across the surface.

Chapter Seven

John kept his mouth shut and his eyes steadfast on the fountain, listening to the others as they tried to unravel the tangled web of events leading them here—sitting in the center of a labyrinth within the hotel. The longer he could keep the attention off himself, the better.

John knew what needed to be done. Although nothing was ever simple in Gem Haven, for once the situation seemed simple enough, since Lavalieres could play a game to the death and be brought back to life. In Gem Haven, people could turn into tigers and wolves...and friends could hide inside a large hedge labyrinth while trying to figure out how to wake up an unconscious girl.

"Are you sure you don't know what Pavlovian is doing with those Lavalieres?" Mark asked and everyone turned to Riley waiting for his response.

"How should I know?" Riley appeared taken aback. "It's not like he's *my* father. Shouldn't you have some idea of what he's up to, Jade?" Riley passed the baton off to her, but she didn't seem any more ready or eager to answer the question than Riley had been.

"I haven't had a single meaningful conversation with my father in forever. I have no clue what he's doing, why there are so many in the hospital wing, or why a statue of my mother exists in a random room I've never seen before." Jade turned away, hiding her face from the others.

"You spend more time hiding from him than speaking to him. Perhaps your mother belongs in there. Maybe she did something as awful as Igneous." Riley's temper had overtaken the conversation.

Even John knew that comment crossed the line. The words stung Jade, whose face had turned a deep shade of blue. The air around them grew cold and frost began to form on the hedges closest to Jade. Ice crystals snaked out over the surface of the water inside the fountain, cracking with their sudden appearance. Riley threw his hands up in protection against the bitter cold.

"Don't you *dare* compare my mother to that man." Jade's eyes glistened in the artificial sunlight. An icy tear dropped off the side of her cheek and shattered against the stone of the fountain.

Riley was going to wind up with an ice dagger through his heart if nobody intervened.

"Calm down there, popsicle. Now isn't the time for us to be turning on each other." Mark stepped in between Jade and Riley, but he didn't act as if he was completely convinced of Riley's innocence in the matter.

The wind picked up, whistling through the branches as dark clouds formed in crashing waves overhead. John placed the palm of his hand against the ground, feeling a noticeable drop in temperature as the soil began to freeze. He jumped to his feet to avoid developing frostbite.

"What are you doing?" Riley yelled, pulling Ruby off the concrete before the ice had a chance to spread beyond the pool. A dull creaking sound could be heard as branches began to lose their integrity bending against the cold. Off in the distance, a loud "snap" as a section of wall broke off and crashed to the ground.

"I'm not doing anything. I swear." Jade threw her hands up in protest. The center of the labyrinth created a vortex of howling wind. John turned to shield himself from the elements, but there was no angle from which he could avoid being assaulted. A roll of thunder rumbled through the darkening clouds.

"Is this normal?" Mark roared over the white noise. The shock on Jade's face made it clear this was in no way normal. Then came the rain. Heavy and cold, the drops splashed against his exposed skin. Even Jade, Ice Girl, was shivering. Her lips turning purple and specks of snowflakes clung to her brow.

Mark and Riley continued to shield Ruby from the elements, with Mark being the more equipped of the two to handle the blasts. John shook. His clothes were soaked thoroughly in mere moments.

"He's trying to flush us out." Riley's teeth chattered as he spoke. "He must have realized you'd bring us here." He cast another accusatory glance at Jade.

"If we're going to get out of this, we have to trust each other." John's outburst surprised even himself, but they were getting nowhere blaming each other. "Jade knows as much about what's happening as we do. Milo isn't a bad guy. At least, I don't think he is. Whatever he and Pavlovian are doing might even be justified. I don't want to give up hope, yet. Only Ruby can help us understand what's happening."

If Pavlovian was on his way to finding them, they couldn't afford to stand around bickering. They needed to act, and fast.

"Even if she knew anything, it's not as if we can ask her," Riley pointed out the major flaw in John's plan. Fortunately, John had already come to the same conclusion and found himself a step ahead of the others.

"She's trapped. You know, in the moment between wake and sleep where the dream feels so real you could convince yourself it is? She's in a terrifying limbo, just on the verge of waking up from a nightmare. I know. I've been there." John shuddered at the idea of putting himself back there. His entire body shook with the combined reaction to the freezing water drenching his skin and his nerves over the thought of what needed to happen next.

"Okay, but we still can't wake her up. We've tried." Riley didn't seem to catch on, but the others were slowly catching up to his train of thought.

"No, but I can get back there." He knew what needed to be done, there was no more stalling. He had to get to her the only way he knew how. He had to tell a lie.

"Everything is going to be okay." He screamed out to the listening universe. He wished he could believe the lie, but everything was falling apart around him.

The complete instant silence of the wind and his friends stunned him, then was instantly replaced by the tunneled emptiness you'd hear if you placed a cup over your ears. The rain ceased, but even more odd was how his clothes were suddenly dry.

The void of the nightmare realm expanded around him, but since the last time he had been here there was a difference. Off in the distance he could make out signs of movement. Multiple entities all moving together in unison, seemingly with purpose. Even the feel of the void against his skin had a new, slightly electric buzz. He waved a hand through the air and felt a small tingling sensation rise through his arm. The hairs on his arm stood on end.

A little ball of light floated up toward him, catching his attention. In the distance, someone pointed in his direction. She dropped to all fours and sprinted toward him. Even if he decided to turn and run, she would outpace him. Not that he wanted to run, she was the reason he came back here in the first place.

"Ruby," he called out, and the wolf came to a halt a short distance away. She reared back on two legs, bones popping as they shifted. Her hairy muzzle receded, revealing the radiant face of the young woman who'd remained unconscious in their care. Her glowing eyes dulled as they widened.

"It's you," she muttered just loud enough for him to hear. A tickle played at the back of John's neck. Much like the rest of the nightmare world, she too had changed. She seemed more alert, more aware of her surroundings.

"You woke me up," said Ruby.

The others who'd been with Ruby, slowly caught up, staying a couple of feet behind her. They formed a small band of maybe six or seven at most.

"No, we weren't able to wake you up, that's why I had to come back here. We tried everything." He worried that he was going to have trouble explaining what was happening. "We're actually back in the…" he paused, his words felt strange on his tongue, "that is we're conscious but not exactly awake."

Was it a trick of the nightmare realm? He couldn't

quite find the words he was looking for.

"The labyrinth...we're, well not all of us...but you're..." He tripped and stumbled over his words, waving his hands as he tried to focus on what he was telling her.

"Don't strain yourself. I understand. I meant you woke me up in this dream. Before you, everything just happened while I followed along, playing out like a movie I couldn't stop watching. Then you came along and woke me up." Her voice was soft and kind.

Ruby waved one of the girls over. She sported a hot pink skirt, had her hair pulled back in tightly braided pigtails and that, combined with a studded lip ring, gave her a "don't mess with me" look. John knew her type. The kind of person who was confident with her appearance and dared others to challenge her style.

"John, meet Abby, she's been helping us track sleepers. She's better than me when it comes to tracking, which is saying something." Ruby caught him up to speed on everything they had learned since he'd disappeared.

"I'm supposed to help transition after waking and assist in acclimating to our current predicament. But as I understand it, you already have some indication of what's going on here." Abby extended her hand for John to shake, and he kept his own introduction short.

"We've learned quite a bit since you woke me up. I've made it my goal to wake up everyone we come across." Ruby indicated the group behind her. John scanned their faces. There was something familiar about them he couldn't quite put his finger on.

"Why do you keep talking about waking up?" John asked. He knew they were still unconscious and, at least the two of them, were still in the labyrinth. A strange sense of familiarity overtook John as he studied the faces of the others. He had seen them before. Then he remembered that they were the Lavalieres he'd seen in the hospital wing. He barely recognized them. The forms they took on here in the dream world all still had full heads of hair.

"Do you know about lucid dreaming?" Abby began, leading John into her tale. "It's called a waking dream, one where you are aware enough to know you are asleep. They can be very powerful." She held up her hand and from it rose a ball of energy, sparking as it rose into the air. She snapped her fingers and it whizzed up into the void before exploding in a cascade of fireworks.

"In a lucid dream, you can do anything your mind can come up with. If you want to fly"—she rose into the air—"you can fly."

Each time they manipulated the void to act in a way they wanted, John felt the static electricity in the air bend and shift. A lot had changed since the last time he'd come here, and his awe of how much control they had over the nightmare realm completely derailed his train of thought.

"We're still looking for others to wake up, if you'd care to join us." Ruby extended her hand in invitation and John found himself joining this peculiar group of aware Lavalieres.

Chapter Eight

John never thought he would want to force himself into the middle of a nightmare, but here he was.

Abby raised her arms and a small bubble of energy formed between her hands. The bubble rose into the air and drifted away from the group. The sudden movement of the collective caught him off guard and he tripped over his feet, stumbling while attempting to keep up with them.

"Here we go again." Ruby devoted her attention to the orb and Abby, moving the group as a unit toward their acquired target.

"There," Abby yelled and pointed out onto the horizon. In the distance, a shaded person he couldn't make out swayed back and forth. Shadows began to gather around him, latching onto his energy.

"Remember, we focus on the nightmare, not the sleeper. Don't let it touch you. Don't let it get into your head. Brace yourselves. Let's go wake him up" Ruby rallied the troops. More than a few appeared unsure of themselves.

"What's going on?" John asked. More than a few of the others in the group had closed their eyes. A calm hush had fallen over them. His words sliced through their meditative state. The deep breathing technique was rhythmic and entrancing. He found himself mimicking their movements. His own breathing slowed as he drew in a long breath. Abby turned to him as the others ignored his question to focus on themselves.

"We can't just rush in there to wake him up. Like waking up a sleepwalker. There can be terrible consequences." She paused, closing her eyes. Her chest rose, shoulders rolling back, "We can do a lot here with just our minds, but so can a sleeper. In order to wake him up, we have to defeat his *nightmare*."

Something about the way she had said the word *nightmare* made a shiver crawl up John's spine.

"What do you mean *defeat*?" he asked as the meditative state he'd been experiencing dissipated into the void. They were preparing themselves for battle, but with what?

"Everyone is afraid of something. Fear can be very powerful on the imagination." Another deep breath in and out. "There are three steps to a successful awakening. One, understand the fear. Two, negate the fear. Three, do not let the fear get its grip on you."

One by one, the others clasped their hands behind their backs. He realized this was a non-verbal indication they were ready to head out. But John wasn't. He still didn't feel like he was fully understanding what they were preparing for.

"We can do anything we want here. We're already lucid dreaming, right?" John couldn't imagine what could be eliciting this kind of reaction from them. When he first saw Ruby and the fire that swept through, threatening to engulf them. Was that her fear? Or was it his?

"Tell me. Say you can do anything you could ever think of. What's the first thing you do?" Abby asked with a half-smile. Her lip ring twitched enthusiastically.

His mind drew a complete blank at the unexpected question. "I...don't know..." he replied.

"We have two theories to explain why. If you can suddenly do anything you ever wanted, our minds are overloaded with possibilities and can't choose just one. The other theory is that this place is actually draining on the imagination. The void is literally nothing, and it's impossible to create something from nothing," Abby explained.

"So you meditate?" He couldn't imagine being able to relax.

"Meditation gets us closer to the dream state where ideas sprout naturally and quickly. Does that make sense?" She took another couple of breaths before joining the others with her hands clasped behind her back.

"I think so." He still wasn't ready, but given he didn't know how long he would remain here, and not wanting to slow the others down, he locked his hands behind his back.

As a unit, they began their journey across the void, toward the sleeping guy. As they moved forward, he thought about what Abby had said, about the imagination becoming dulled here.

He'd spent a good portion of his life walking among his own daydreams, never fitting in well enough with real life to maintain a large circle of friends. He could conjure up entire worlds at whim, inhabiting them with all kinds of people and creatures that could only exist in a child's mind. Even though that had changed since he became a Lavaliere and met his new friends, the fantasies and dreaming hadn't completely disappeared from his life.

But here, this was different. He had to push himself to come up with even a single imaginative thought, and even then, he could feel the ideas dissipating…like they were floating away on the breeze. He was began to feel a lot less confident in his ability to cast away whatever nightmare they were about to be thrown into.

As difficult as it was to form even a single interesting thought, on the opposite end of the spectrum, it was way too easy for him to think about what he would least like to face. He pictured a dark robe and the sunken eyes of a monster glaring out from under a hood.

"Do you feel that?" Abby whispered.

He did. The world around them grew hot with the buzz of electricity in the air. The others tensed, causing John's stomach to tighten involuntarily. There was still a considerable distance between them and the sleeper. His heartbeat began to pound in his chest. The suspense and slow pace made him worry he was somehow going to mess up their process.

The void pulled in, wrapping shrouds and wisps in swirls of pure nothing. His mind locked in on the ribbons of black, knowing full well what was forming from those horrific remnants of thought. As much as he wished he could cast away the solidified images in his head, they refused to remain repressed. They took root, like a seed planted deep into his subconscious.

The man, tall and menacing, rose out of the ground. John's breathing pace quickened. pace. The others had no idea just how powerful this nightmare was. The worst part was that John knew his own memories were feeding the monster, making him stronger. This wasn't the sleeper's nightmare. It was his.

The others had no clue how much trouble they were in. Igneous was not the kind of man he wanted to tango with on more than one occasion. They'd barely contained him the first time, and now he wasn't even real. This version of Igneous wasn't constrained and limited by the physical world. In here, his power could draw on the void, making him far more deadly.

They were all physically located inside of Gem Haven still, but that fact did nothing to quell John's fears. Would the Lavaliere protection Pavlovian placed over the hotel keep them safe? His body would regenerate if severely damaged, but there was no telling what would happen to his mind if he were attacked here in the nightmare realm. At best, he might wake back up with his friends. At worst, he could wind up comatose like Ruby and Abby and the others. Or maybe even worse, what if he wound up completely unconscious, floating in this void for eternity? He shuddered at the thought.

John blinked. The world around him felt like it could cave in on him without a moment's notice. He opened his mouth to warn the others, and then all hell broke loose. A bolt of plasma whizzed toward Igneous, who absorbed the energy and reflected the blast back at the group. Everyone scattered, split up by the attack. John needed to think fast, he needed to come up with any kind of plan to contain this monster. His mind was blank, too busy focusing on survival instead of winning.

Igneous let out a roar, and fire flew from his mouth, setting the world ablaze with its intense heat. The external flame encircled them, herding the group together, and cutting them off from the rest of the void. Igneous laughed menacingly. He stood between them and the sleeper.

John's body temperature rose with every lick of flame. The surrounding warmth comforted him in a way he'd only known from one other person. Milo. If Milo were here, he'd know how to handle Igneous. He'd have a plan to get them out of this terrible situation in a pinch. Milo may have changed, but there was no way he would allow his friends to be in any real danger. John knew this to be true down to his very soul.

All around him the battle waged, kids he'd only just met throwing everything they could imagine at a monster larger than life itself. And yet, John found himself growing calm.

Finally, he could answer Abby's question. If he could have anything in the world, it would be Milo. He wanted his best friend back.

He embraced the warmth, letting heat envelope him, wrapping around him like a blanket. Still with his eyes closed, he pictured Milo's smiling face. No matter what he was up to, John could never let go of his love.

"I'll always be here for you," Milo whispered, and John opened his eyes. His heart performed multiple backflips as he wrapped his arms around the boy in front of him. He hoped beyond anything that the guy in front of him wasn't just an illusion formed from his imagination. The embrace certainly felt real enough.

Igneous turned away from the others, ignoring their struggling attacks. His eyes burned like coal, the hood of his robe falling off to reveal the Diadem hidden beneath. Milo turned to stare down the monster.

"Zack?" Abby yelled, using the opportunity to bypass the distracted Igneous.

Like her, many others deserted the original nightmare to focus on the sleeper. Milo stood steadfast between John and his foe.

Now that he had a champion on his side, John felt a lot better about his odds of getting through this challenge.

Milo reached his hand out into the fire and pulled forth a burning sword, emblazoned with a design of flames snaking from the hilt to the tip. The molten metal glowed a pinkish red. Milo swung the mighty blade in an arc, sending a beam of flame hurtling toward Igneous. It cut through the void, creating a hole that filled in as fast as it had formed.

"No." A scream came from the sleeper. The effect of Milo's slice appeared to be minimal to the nightmare, but whatever he'd done had stirred a major reaction from the sleeper.

Chapter Nine

John was awestruck at the sight before him. Milo took on the appearance of a knight, majestic and strong in the face of danger. He brandished the mighty sword, extending it as though it was a part of his own body. Flame licked the sharp blade up to the tip where embers sparked with anticipation of being used.

Shadow Igneous locked eyes on John's protector. A bubbling mass of void oozed up from the ground, forming a sleek blade of dark energy. A gray mist swirled around the hilt, cracking with small bursts of lightning.

Milo squared off with the monster, formed from the void and shadows of the nightmare realm, and empowered by the warped, unrealistic images floating in John's head.

The diadem shimmered on top of Igneous' skull. Even if it wasn't real, it was still menacing. John caught sight of Milo's bloodstone set in the center. Milo swung and the two blades met with a furious blast of energy.

"You are worthless," the monster hissed. With their swords locked together, the bloodstone activated. The flames around Milo's sword sputtered like a candle on an open windowsill. As they died out, Igneous only grew more powerful. He pushed Milo back.

Tendrils of the void shot from the end of Igneous' sword, snaking their way toward Milo and John. Milo sliced in a downward arc, a line of fire bursting from the blade and lighting the void ablaze.

"Stop," the sleeper continued to scream. With his eyes clamped shut, he began to rock back and forth. Abby and Ruby were already at his side, doing everything in their power to wake him up and end this nightmare.

Milo slashed away at the strands of the void. He shuffled back as they continued to advance despite his efforts.

John's guilt overpowered his senses, taking control of his body, constricting him as he lay on the ground. He was useless, always making situations far worse than they were to begin with.

No matter where he went, or how he tried to help, his simply being there seemed to put others in danger. What use was it being a Lavaliere with any kind of gift if it only served to make things worse?

John was responsible for Milo losing his powers after the big battle with the real Igneous. He failed at realizing Milo had been under Igneous' control because of the bloodstone, and it nearly cost them their lives. If not because of his need to get out of the hotel, they never would have been chased away from the diner and he wouldn't have lied. His friends wouldn't be trapped in the middle of a labyrinth with two unconscious bodies to protect after being chased. And he wouldn't have been able to create this monstrous void creature from his over-the-top imagination.

The void advanced and wrapped around Milo's wrist, forcing the sword to clatter to the ground. Milo's eyes went wide as one wrapped itself around his neck and began to squeeze the life out of him.

John let out a scream of frustration and wrenched himself up off the ground. *This is my fault.* John projected Milo's pain onto himself. He could feel the void wrapped around his own neck, squeezing tight.

Milo showed very little sign of his own struggling, but John could see Milo's lips turning a deep shade of purple. John clenched his fist in anger and pain.

"You don't exist. Go away." The truth of John's words rang heavy through the arena. His powerful suggestion appeared to catch the monster off guard. The void retreated back to its source. Milo fell to the ground, gasping for his next breath. Igneous reared up, flames streaming from his neck. He flew high up into the air.

"You failed me," Igneous said. The sleeper dropped to the ground as the nightmare spun into a ball of void and darted away, disappearing in the distance. With the monster's departure, the firewall surrounding them faded.

John stood there in shock. He'd done it. They'd won the battle. Igneous went away and the sleeper had awoken, but the ordeal left him feeling somewhat empty.

"What did you do?" Ruby demanded breaking the silence. John didn't realize she was talking to him at first. He scrambled to come up with a good enough response.

"Defeated the nightmare?" he tried. He knew immediately it wasn't the response she was looking for.

"They don't just fly away. I've never seen a nightmare continue to exist after waking the sleeper." Abby's tone felt slightly accusatory.

"You need to prepare yourself," Milo said. He

appeared to be the only one not completely shaken up over the ordeal. John could have used a bit of Milo's stoic resolve in that moment.

"He's just a memory, a figment of the imagination. He'll have fallen apart by now," Ruby said with a hint of apprehension.

"Milo. If you hurt my father, I'll kill you." Zack was no longer sitting idly on the sidelines. Milo raised his hand and the ground around Zack rose up and latched onto his legs, trapping him where he stood.

"I didn't turn your father into a monster. He did that on his own." He turned away from Zack and addressed Ruby, "As for who I am, I'm the only person who can save you all. But, I need to know where you are."

"Nice to see you again, Milo," Abby said, to John's surprise. The two of them knew each other, but John didn't recognize her or Zack from any of his dreams. "We're in some kind of dream realm. Paul has been getting worse and while I struggled to locate a cure, I managed to get myself stuck here and have been trying to find a way back for a while now."

"Good to see you too, Abby, just wish it were under better circumstances. Forgive me, but I'm not concerned about where we are mentally, I really need to know where John and the others took Ruby."

"That's really all you care about?" John suddenly felt apprehensive. Milo had come to save him without hesitation, but it might not have been as selfless as it first appeared.

"No." The scream turned into a long, drawn out wail. They put their conversation on hold to rush over to see what the problem was, and found another member of the group huddled over an unconscious body. The boy on the ground wasn't moving. His eyes were partially open, but he didn't appear to be breathing.

"What happened here?" Ruby asked as she knelt down next to the guy.

"He was attacked by the nightmare. The void went straight through his heart. I thought he'd wake up, but he isn't responding to anything."

"He's got no pulse. How is this possible?" Ruby's shoulders sagged. Everybody avoided asking the most difficult question. Was he truly gone?

"This is why I need to know where you are. With Igneous on the loose in here, nobody is safe." Milo placed his hand on John's arm.

John had missed the caring touch of his best friend for the past couple of days.

Milo waved his hand and the ground shifted, cracking around them as it opened up and swallowed the dead body of their friend. A small mound remained when it finished. For John, the resemblance it bore to a burial plot broke him.

"He's okay though, right? The hotel will protect him from harm." John turned away as he said this, not wanting to look upon the grave any longer than he had to. He'd never even thought to take the time to learn any of their names. The fact hadn't even crossed his mind prior to now.

"No, I'm sorry, he's gone." Milo stepped away from the grave and a heavy silence fell over the group. "You guys need to be a lot more careful from here on out. Whatever happens in here has very real repercussions out there." Milo's words covered the group like a thick blanket in the middle of summer, useful and generally protective, but now instilled a sense of discomfort.

John couldn't help but feel like there was more to all of this and Milo was withholding information. He'd managed to fall within an area of telling the truth, but only just, so many times now that John was beginning to question the reliability in every statement. On the other hand, paranoia had a tendency to run rampant when he could no longer trust his own instincts. After all, Milo had helped get rid of the shadow version of Igneous.

"I can help you all, but doing so requires John to tell me where he is." Milo turned to John, a pleading look in his eyes. If John gave up their position, Pavlovian was sure to find them, but if he refused then he'd be turning his back on his friend.

From what he gathered in his short conversations with Ruby, she didn't know much more about what was happening to all of them than he did. If he really wanted answers, it seemed as though he'd have to go directly to the source. On top of everything, he didn't get the indication that Milo was lying about being able to help everyone.

With his mind made up, he couldn't help but wonder how he was going to explain his decision to Riley, Mark, and Jade. They would likely never forgive him for giving up their position, but enough was enough. He had to think of the well-being of these Lavalieres above his own.

"We're in the middle of Jade's labyrinth." He offered up the information, hoping he'd made the right choice in the given circumstances. He couldn't take the risk of Igneous coming back and harming anyone else.

"Let me go," Zack yelled, still confined to Milo's trap.

"Be careful with him, that monster we fought was his father." Milo waved his hand and freed Zack from the prison. John's eyes went wide with realization. They just helped wake up the son of the man who tried to kill them. Igneous didn't form just from his thoughts alone. They must have fed into the sleepers, creating a super-powered nightmare.

"I'll kill you." Zack once again bolted toward Milo. As he got close, he jumped with arms outstretched. He would have knocked him to the ground if Milo hadn't suddenly disappeared from where he'd been standing only to reappear a couple feet to his left. Zack landed hard on the ground with a grunt.

"Try to keep each other safe." Milo's words served as both encouragement and warning. Without saying another word, he disappeared.

"Who was that?" Ruby asked.

"Milo. He became a Lavaliere at the same time I did," Abby replied. "I should probably mention, he's a leech." Abby seemed apprehensive to provide the final detail, almost like she wanted to protect him, but her loyalty to this group outweighed whatever friendship they had.

"Not anymore. We had to remove the bloodstone because Igneous was using it to control him." John, like Abby, wasn't sure just how much information he wanted to share about Milo.

"Don't you dare talk bad about my father," Zack demanded. "Milo is a filthy leech."

"Doesn't matter to me. He helped us. And given

our situation, I'm willing to trust anybody who wants to help." Ruby turned to Zack and said, "Including you if you're willing to lose the attitude."

"Why would I join you? I can take care of myself." Zack brushed himself off and crossed his arms in front of his chest.

"Because even if he was your father, he is still also your nightmare. Meaning you're afraid of him. And since you brought him into this world from your imagination, you'll be his target. The real question you should be asking is, why are we so willing to help you out when you've been nothing but trouble? The answer is because we are above pettiness. We help those who need help. Sticking together is the best way to survive this place. But by all means, if you think you'll be better off alone, be my guest." Ruby held her hand up, giving Zack the opportunity to sever himself from the group.

Zack dropped his arms in reluctant defeat, falling into place with the rest of them. Ruby may have been willing to give him a chance, but John could already see a few of the others were hesitant to accept him so easily.

Chapter Ten

"We've never faced anything so strong before." Ruby lamented, she had been unable to rally her troops after the harrowing battle with Igneous. Up until now, waking someone up had meant searching, understanding their fears, and then conquering them. It was a game, one they had been fairly good at given the size of the group.

But now they had lost one of their own. His name was Danny, and his gemstone was the emerald. John made a point of getting to know the others, at least their names and gems if nothing more. Jessica—Diamond. Nichole—Sapphire. Lyle—another Emerald. Ruby—Tiger's Eye. Abby—Amethyst. Hannah—Ruby. And so on. There was no way he was going to be able to commit it all to memory, but he felt better at least trying. As he had expected, many of them fell into the category of *precious* gem users. Zack was the only person who refused to offer up any of his own information.

"Igneous is bad news. He's powerful because he had been collecting powers using the Diadem." John told them all about the battle and how Igneous had been using Milo to get to Jade. Every time Milo's name was mentioned, Zack would let out an audible huff. Clearly the two of them didn't get along.

"You're all ignorant. Blinded by the fool

Pavlovian. My father wouldn't have done what he did if it wasn't absolutely necessary." Zack's face had gone deep red, his chest pumping up and down as he spewed his discontent.

"Please, by all means, tell us why he was forced to poison gem bonds, steal Lavaliere powers, and manipulate people in order to attack groups. This *thing* might not really be him, but I'm sure it classifies as just as evil. If you were so afraid of him, why are you defending him?" John couldn't contain his patience any longer. Familial bond aside, there was no denying the amount of harm this one man caused to so many.

"You think Pavlovian was rounding up Lavalieres to keep them protected from my dad? You are so very narrow minded if you think the world is as big as your backyard." Zack spat his venom, attacking the character of the man who claimed he was keeping them safe. John couldn't allow himself to stoop to throwing jabs back and forth with Zack. He came here for information, and he was determined to get it in one shape or another.

"You don't even know the first thing about the schism of the high council, do you?" Zack interrupted. He looked like he wasn't going to settle down until he could get everything off his chest.

"Schism? What's a schism?" Ruby asked, prompting Zack to continue. John found himself silenced, forced to go with the new flow of the conversation.

"A schism is when there's a division within a group or organization. Both my father and Pavlovian used to be on the high council until they were cast out. Pavlovian wanted to build an army of Lavalieres, even went out of his way to start manufacturing them, starting with his own daughter. He's been bringing you all there to join him in his own quest for power."

"It's not like that at all," John protested. Even though he couldn't fully vouch for Pavlovian's character based on what he'd witnessed, he couldn't stretch his imagination far enough to believe he was building an army.

"Think about it, one person gathering tons of the strongest Lavalieres all into one place. He wants you on his side when the war begins. My father had to go through some extreme measures to infiltrate the base, sure, but he's not the one you should really fear." Zack held the seed of doubt out there for him to take.

"Pavlovian asked me to join him a while back, when I first got my gem. I only started getting attacked by Augers after I turned him down." Ruby turned away from him. John didn't want to think the two scenarios were connected, correlation doesn't prove causation. Auger attacks were becoming much more frequent lately, probably just a coincidence. However, the seed had taken root, and now John was beginning to question Pavlovian and some of the other choices that had been made.

"If he could get away with it, I bet he'd have you guys training in combat." Zack smirked when John didn't have a proper reply.

John bit his tongue. Technically, they been training. In a combat-type environment. That was the whole point of the game Gembreakers. Pit two teams against each other in a test of power.

With how easily Jade took to engaging in confrontations, it would be difficult to make a counter claim. Gembreakers was passed off as a method to teach them how to use their abilities, but was it more than that? Even if he didn't want them to, the pieces were beginning to fit together all too well.

"I never felt like he could be trusted, which is why I'll never step foot inside the safe haven he created." Ruby's statement caused John to perk up. He bit his lip, wishing he'd been able to speak with her sooner.

"About that. Actually, we brought you back to the hotel after we found you." John hoped to get the information out there as fast as possible, as if he was confessing to a horrible deed.

"He kept trying to convince me I needed to come to Gem Haven. I'm sure whatever is going on now isn't going to change his mind in the slightest." Ruby shook her head. She didn't seem happy, but wasn't flying off the handle either, which was a great relief for John.

"I used to like the idea we could do anything here, but dreams aren't meant to go on forever. Can you help us get out of here?" The plea came from the girl still on the ground.

A general consensus ebbed through the group. The battle with Igneous had changed them, taking away their innocence and turning their lighthearted adventure into a dark journey.

"I want to help. It's why I came back. The problem is I got here by a different means than all of you. I'm only stuck temporarily," John explained. He suddenly realized everyone's eyes were on him, he'd once again found himself the center of attention, and he began to panic. His breath shortened, a bubble of anxiety formed in his chest.

"Now that you're back, maybe you could lead us?

After all, you were the one who woke me up. I've just been waking the others up since you left," Ruby suggested, putting him on spot.

Why couldn't they all just go back to talking amongst themselves? Ruby was a great leader, and it wasn't as if he knew any more about this place than they did. His vision tunneled as he tried to keep his cool. A low rumbling surfaced from the ground below as the world vibrated. Bubbles and cracks spilled up through the ground, tremors containing small void bubbles. It was the distraction he needed, enough to pull the other's attention away from him. But now there was this new problem. *Pop.* Void bubbles oozed through the cracks, rising up into the air.

Another low rumble and a circular crack formed around John, the ground rumbling as it rose up, creating a small pedestal. His mind latched onto a single memory and he felt the world shifting to work around his thoughts, to make them real. Three pillars rose out of the ground, himself standing on top of the tallest. Then three more pillars rose a short distance away.

"John, stop. You're doing this," Ruby yelled from ground level. Being singled out as the reason did nothing to help ease John's anxiety. His pillar kept rising the more he urged it to lower. His fear took over, driving him higher into the never-ending sky. He did the only thing he could think of, he clenched his eyes shut. But that didn't stop the rush of air around him.

"John, take a deep breath, calm down." Ruby's voice made her sound as though she were right next to him, but that wouldn't have been possible. She continued to speak, her voice soft and slow. He listened, keeping his eyes shut, and he followed each and every one of her instructions, until finally it felt as though the pillar had stopped moving. He slowly and cautiously opened his eyes.

"Good job," said Ruby as she floated beside the pillar. John's eyes went wide. She was flying. Even though he'd seen it earlier, he still had difficulty wrapping his head around the concept of being able to do anything here. A warmth spread over him. She stayed right there with him the entire time. He had difficulty finding the words to thank her. She just smiled.

"How high up are we?" He dreaded finding out the answer.

"Only as high up as you think you are," she replied casually. John sighed and worked up the courage to look over the edge. On the ground below, he was still close enough to see the group, but far enough away that they wouldn't be able to hear even if they yelled down.

"I guess you really aren't the leader type." Ruby giggled, certainly not the lighthearted response he was expecting after such an event.

He shivered and shook his head. He would much rather blend in with the background and let others take control. Ruby was that person, the one everyone could gather around for strength and direction.

"I hope you aren't afraid of heights." Ruby cocked her head to the side with a hopeful smile.

"Not particularly." John was far more nervous about being the center of attention than standing atop a giant pillar.

"You had a question for me earlier, would you feel more comfortable if we talk up here?"

John realized Ruby was beginning to discover he

wasn't the deity she made him out to be. No, he knew he was a coward. He nodded. Maybe being up here alone was the best for the moment.

"Do you remember anything about the attack?" The question had taken a back seat to everything else going on, but without everyone cutting him off, he was finally able to get back around to asking. "We don't know much out there and any information you have might help lead us to a solution."

He shifted on the pillar, giving just enough room for Ruby to land. Her face scrunched up, and she ran her hands through her thin hair, pulling all of it to one side. Ruby closed her eyes and the air around them grew thick. Wisps of foggy mist swirled in like clouds at their feet. The calm serenity helped melt the tension he'd built up. His shoulders relaxed, and his eyes fell upon a small shadow forming amongst the mist.

The shadow took on the form of a small wolf. John knew not to be afraid. The coy wolf crept over, and John hesitantly reached out to pet the incorporeal canine.

When the two joined, a surge of energy flowed through John unlike any he'd felt before. The shadow pulled up inside him and bestowed a powerful memory. John allowed Ruby's memory to play out, as though he had lived through it personally.

The visual opened up on a dense forest. There were others, he could sense them, but he couldn't see them. He knew he was looking out through his friend's eyes, seeing everything she had seen. He reached out and touched the monitor, getting pulled inside.

Chapter Eleven

John found himself pulled inside Ruby's memory. All of his senses were firing at a magnitude far beyond normal. In her memory, he felt more connected to the earth than ever.

He drew in a deep breath, picking up new and unique scents, there were so many it was difficult to categorize them all. Pollen, nectar, dirt, animal. And food.

He could see. Everything. The smallest details of the notches and lines in the pine trees. The stark red body of a cardinal perched on a branch a good forty feet away. But he couldn't see the source of the food.

And the sounds, the forest was completely alive with the sounds of skittering animals and the wind as it forced its way around each piece of this balanced ecosystem. But one sound was missing. And another, the bungling gait of an inexperienced cub.

His head snapped around and locked on another wolf. Strange. *Another* wolf. This other wolf was smaller, her coat was as black as night, her eyes golden like the moon. She held her front paw slightly raised, her head cocked to the side the same way a child would if they thought they were in trouble.

Ruby huffed and turned away from the cub, raising her head to sniff the air. The scent of food was growing stronger. His ears focused, listening for the missing cries of a dying deer. *Snap.* John's attention turned to the cub, his focus as broken as the twig beneath Felicia's paw.

"I'm sorry. I don't seem to have the same instincts as you." She pulled back, ashamed with herself. A sense of impatience flowed through John and he realized he was feeling what Ruby was feeling.

"It's okay Felicia. This is only your first transformation. The point isn't to be perfect. It's to show you the freedom that comes with it."

"But why must we hunt? Can't we just go for a run or a swim or something?" Felicia sat down on her hind legs. Her cute innocence was almost too much for John to handle. He wanted to give in to her every whim. Whatever she wanted to do was fine by him.

Ruby shook her head to cast out those thoughts.

"You are really strong. You almost had me convinced there. You're going to make a great alpha. We have to hunt. Our bodies need the food." Ruby's eyes narrowed, she was already feeling the first signs of slipping. Her head lowered, whiskers twitching. It was the animal inside of her trying to convince her this cub was somehow an enemy.

"We must hunt," she said, regaining some control over herself. "If we don't, we risk hurting the ones we love."

"I would never hurt my family or friends," the cub protested, speaking with an air of innocence.

John nearly puked at the putrid taste of her lie.

"Maybe not on purpose, but without sustenance, your feral form will overpower you. You won't be able keep your human mind active." The warning was clear and it appeared as though the cub took it to heart. Ruby refused to hunt at first, doing everything in her power to keep from performing the task associated with her most basic instinct.

Her inner wolf had taken over, starved and alone, she had been forced to watch as her wolf stalked its prey. An overwhelming sense of sadness fell over John. He was certain he now knew how Riley had gotten his scars.

John wanted to know more, to better understand Ruby's pain and concern, but the memory was pushed aside to pursue the task at hand. For her, it was better this way, to separate herself from everyone she could potentially harm and create a small pack. They could hunt and run and be free.

"I think I smell something, over there?" The cub's head moved forward, nose pointing in a direction deeper in the woods

Ruby lifted her nose and sniffed, trying to pick up on it, the scent she'd lost earlier.

John felt every grain of soft, wet dirt beneath Ruby's paws. Each of her wolf senses were on high alert. The other wolf, Felicia, fell in line. Her body tensed behind Ruby's, and the two of them took off through the woods. Their pace quickened and slowed, changing in tiny ways to account for the change in terrain and a multitude of other factors.

John couldn't mentally keep up with the reasons behind many of the decisions Ruby made, but luckily, he didn't need to. Like everything else, this played out like a movie for him, moving him right along with the action. The wolves split from the scent, choosing instead to take a path around a small clearing, leaped over a small river, and then doubled back a bit before picking up the scent and the chase once more.

Then Ruby stopped. It wasn't a planned stop. She wouldn't even be able to explain why, but there was something about their nearby meal that made her feel a bit uneasy. Felicia barreled into her at full speed from behind and the two of them crashed into a nearby shrub. The sound resonated off the canopy walls and echoed for quite a distance. Afterward, nothing but silence.

"Why did you stop?" Felicia asked, whining like a child who just let a balloon escape. The sound of the crash must have scared away any animal in the vicinity, no matter how injured they were. And yet, the scent was still very strong in the cool air.

"I'm not sure," she replied, hesitantly pulling herself back up off the ground. Her stomach rumbled, the overwhelming scent driving her urge to hunt.

"Come on, let's get this over with." The young cub's commanding tone overrode Ruby's senses. Maybe the animal they were chasing was dead already. That would explain why it hadn't run away.

"Of course," Ruby replied without hesitation. Even against her better senses, this cub had an inexplicable power over her. The two of them continued forward. The scent was far stronger than any Ruby had encountered in the past.

They walked out into a small, empty clearing. Ruby's eyes locked on to the dead center, right where the scent would be the strongest. She knew the animal should have been there, they'd detoured for that very reason, to get a better sense of the location of the meat.

Everything inside John screamed this was wrong, but his head couldn't put the pieces together.

Had it gotten away? He couldn't be sure. Ruby

made her way to the center of the clearing. *Snap.* Had Felicia stepped on another twig? But the ground here was all soft and springy, and nothing should have made that noise. Ruby turned to see the smaller wolf fumbling. Backing up, the trap released from under her paw, and a cage dropped down onto them from above.

"Gotcha." A man wearing camouflage clothing, drenched in the scent Ruby had picked up, came out from behind a nearby tree.

"Please, sir, help me. You trapped me in here with a dangerous wolf." Felicia's human voice fell dull on Ruby's senses. Ruby turned to her companion, but the wolf had already shifted back into her human form. What was she doing? John felt the confusion washing over Ruby. She growled, realizing the girl was going to get herself free. It was too late for Ruby to shift back. The hunter had already seen her in wolf form.

"How the…It's a kid. Stay calm. I'll get you out of there." The hunter raised his gun, taking aim at Ruby.

"Stay." Felicia's command washed over Ruby, forcing her to remain still. She caught sight of a sparkling gem attached to the chain around Felicia's neck. To her surprise, it wasn't a tiger's eye. It was pure and clear, a perfectly cut diamond. A loud *POP* accompanied a force against her chest. She looked down and saw a small feather tipped arrow sticking out of her fur. The world around her began to spin.

"It's a tranquilizer, it will put her to sleep, and I'll be able to get you out of there safely." The hunter ran up to the cage.

Ruby wished she had the strength to turn herself back, to tell the hunter she wasn't an animal. Instead, her head hit the floor.

She blinked, unable to recall what had happened or where she was. It wasn't until she saw the bars on the trap that she remembered the hunter and the dart. She scrambled to pull herself up off the ground and checked, but there was no tranquilizer.

"Thank you for all of your help. You were quite an excellent teacher." Felicia's voice was still full of sweet innocence. Ruby, still groggy, tried to follow where the sound was coming from. Felicia sat just outside the cage, beyond arms' reach. The diamond still around her neck, reflecting a ray of sun that peeked in through the canopy.

The hunter sat at her feet, looking content with himself. Ruby lifted herself up and transformed back to her human form. The transformation was slow and a bit painful, but as she shifted, the effects of the tranquilizer wore off.

"What happened?" she asked.

John couldn't take his eyes off of Felicia's. They maintained the moonlike glow, a small reminder of her other form. A smirk splayed across her smug face.

"He shot you. I thought he was aiming to kill. That would have helped me out in the long run. Unfortunately, it wasn't the case. Was it, boy?" She turned and gave the hunter a pat on the head. The man barked playfully.

"What did you do to him?" Ruby slammed her hands on the bars of the cage. The metal bars vibrated underneath.

John felt her anger bubbling up within. He wanted to lash out at the girl who betrayed them. He couldn't help but take it as a personal blow. He'd trusted her. No, Ruby trusted her. He had to remind himself this was still just a memory, something that already happened.

"Isn't it obvious? I made him a lapdog. Anyway, sorry I can't stick around, but I have errands to run. As for you, *sleep.*" Ruby's eyes felt heavy, and she had trouble keeping them open. The command washed over her, and made her want to obey.

John stumbled back, pulling himself out of the memory. Ruby stood beside him, a sad look on her face. He had no idea this was what she was running away from. All he could do was pull her into a tight hug.

"But wait, we were told Augers were behind this." John pulled away in shocked realization. This was the key piece of information he needed to take back to Riley.

"I've been forcing myself not to think about it. I trusted her. I really thought we were friends." Ruby turned away, looking down on the group below, a group of Lavalieres she'd found and befriended. She needed them, and they needed her.

John was about to ask how they were going to get down from there when he felt a strange tugging on his arm. He looked down, but nothing was there. Then, a pressure pushed against his chest, and he felt his body shake.

"Come on, you need to wake up." He heard the words as a faint whisper on the wind. It sounded familiar, but he couldn't quite place the voice. The pillar swayed, and he failed at maintaining his balance. Another tug on his arm and he lost his footing, tumbling backward off the slab.

"John," Ruby screamed. Her voice mixed with

others, all calling out to him. His head went dizzy, air rushing by him as he plummeted toward the ground. For a brief moment, he panicked. Ruby was flying toward him, but she wouldn't be fast enough. He closed his eyes and braced himself for impact.

There was a moment as he was falling when his mind and body felt as though they were split between two different places. His mind was still falling, but his body was perfectly still. This disconnect brought about a twitch in his muscles as they all tensed up at the same time.

Chapter Twelve

John had to shield his eyes. The walls of the hedge rose up around him. The rain had stopped, traded for the stinging rays of an oversized sun. All around him, the ground steamed and sizzled.

John groaned and wiped away sticky sweat from his forehead. His body was hot throughout, and even though the sun beating down on his exposed skin was a fake one, it still felt like it could leave a nasty burn.

He could remember the events of the nightmare, but like with every dream, they felt distant and impossible. Details became fuzzy and blurred together, distancing himself from the events, as though they had only occurred in his own mind.

"John, are you okay?" Riley's short breath made his words heavy and slow. They still appeared to be in the center of the labyrinth, but all of the conditions had changed. John quickly tried to assess what was happening. Even the hedge walls appeared to be sweating in the sauna like conditions.

If the cold rain and wind were to draw them out of their hiding place, this intense heat was obviously meant to keep them in place.

Jade sat with her back against the base of the dry fountain, all of the water inside it evaporated away. Her mouth hung open, face glistening and dripping. Her shirt was drenched and her eyes were rolling back in her head. If anyone should have been checked on, it was her. She looked like death.

"Yeah, I'm fine." He struggled to force himself into a sitting position, his muscles not wanting to respond. Mark lounged, a lump of orange fur on the ground, pressed up against the side of the hedge in order to try to find the little bit of shade he could.

"You passed out, and then started shaking and convulsing, we thought you were having a seizure. What happened?" Riley pulled off his shirt, wrung it out, and then wrapped it around his neck.

"I had to get myself to the nightmare realm, that's where they are all trapped, walking through a shared dream." John paused, lethargy setting in.

"You found her? You spoke with my sister?" Riley had a renewed sense of energy as he understood what John was implying.

"Yeah, they're trapped," he repeated, hoping to get the point across. "But it's worse than that, we unleashed a monster. Igneous is back." Everybody jumped at the news. A staggering difference in reaction now that he was among those who actually knew and understood the severity of the problem.

"Is she okay?" Riley pulled back, his face showing his disbelief. John nodded.

"What do you mean he's back? Not possible, he's a statue," Mark growled.

"If he can come back, do you think my mom could as well?" Jade's concern was overshadowed by her disillusioned hope at regaining her family.

Their response was a bit overwhelming for him. Each had their own priorities. He didn't know where to start or how to answer everyone's questions all at once.

Every time he attempted, they threw a dozen more at him. His train of thought was derailed so many times he began to lose focus on what was important and what still needed clarification.

"It's true, he's back." Milo stepped into the center of the labyrinth. John wasn't sure if he believed his friend was real, or just a mirage due to the heat.

Riley and Jade readied themselves for a fight. Mark seemed unsure of himself, much like John. The two of them were friends with everyone here and didn't want to see anyone fight.

"Wait, I told him we were here." John said, hoping to ease some of the tension.

"Why would you lead him here?" Riley turned his anger on John.

"He did it because it was the right thing to do," Milo replied, bringing himself farther into the center. He glanced at Ruby, laying still, back on the ledge of the fountain. He put on a fake smile, acting as though there were nothing wrong with the picture.

For a few tense moments, nobody said a word. As if they each expected that by starting the conversation, they would be the ones to cause an end to this standoff. John was directly in the center of it all.

"Milo showed up when Igneous was attacking us, he helped keep us safe before I drove him away." John tried to help them understand.

"And all of this happened while you were unconscious?" Mark asked. The stares he was getting gave him the impression they all thought he was insane. But there was no denying how Milo knew exactly where to go after he'd told him in the nightmare realm.

"Mark, you know me, I can't lie without slipping

back into that *place*. Igneous is back, at least the memory of him is. It's my fault." John finally had the opportunity to explain what he knew about the dream world and all that happened while he was there.

"It's not your fault. Felicia is manipulating the nightmares. She's trying to bring him back," Milo assured him.

"And how do you play into all of this?" Riley asked. "What were you doing in the hospital wing with all of those Lavalieres?"

"It's a long story I'm not sure we have time for. We need to get Ruby back, and the others could be in trouble. John, will you help me? We need to move Ruby back to the hospital wing as soon as possible." Milo's insistence tugged at John. Milo was using their relationship and him in order to get what he wanted.

"No," John said simply. He couldn't allow this to continue without any explanations. "You owe us. I won't do anything until you explain yourself. You've been leaving every single night without so much as a word about where you're going. You evaded me and your friends, stretched the truth, and betrayed my trust by taking and reading my diary. If you want us to help you, you're going to have to rebuild our trust."

Speaking with little regard to what he was saying or how it would be taken, John held back tears as he locked eyes with Milo. He'd never felt so strong, not even when defeating Igneous for the second time. He teetered on the edge of a breakdown, but none of that mattered. What mattered was getting his friend back. He wanted the deceit to end. He needed Milo to tell him everything.

"Jade?" Mark ran over to her side, in the time they

were focused on Milo she had slumped over shaking on the ground. Her face was beet red, lips quivering.

How could he have been so stupid? John immediately should have realized that this heat would cause major problems for an ice user, similarly to how Milo had a problem with the cold.

Everyone was reacting poorly to the conditions, but she would be accustomed to the cold. Heat was her disability, and if it were anything like his own, she would find herself in the nightmare realm.

"We have to get her out of these conditions. She needs shade." Riley began pulling at the sides of the hedge maze, tearing off leaves and vines, but nothing substantial enough to provide cover for Ruby. Milo was the only one who didn't appear to be suffering from the heat, likely a lingering side effect of his original abilities from being a bloodstone Lavaliere.

Clouds were already starting to move in overhead blocking the sun's harsh rays. John didn't feel the difference at first. The temperature began to drop back to livable.

A collective sigh of relief emanated amongst the group as they tugged at their still sweaty and sticky shirts. Even with the cooling temperature, Jade didn't look much better. If anything, her breathing had quickened and more sweat glistened across her forehead.

"Now, we need to get Ruby back and hooked up." Milo insisted and John's shoulders dropped. Milo's attempt to capitalize on the distraction struck a nerve in John.

"Why are you avoiding answering our questions?" John asked outright, knowing if Milo tried to dodge this time, he'd be able to call him on it.

"Because you wouldn't understand," Milo snapped back. John wasn't sure how to respond. He knew Milo firmly believed in his statement, there wasn't even the slightest hint of insincerity.

"I disagree, we're your friends and we will help you no matter what, but the only way we can is if you include us." John remembered how Ruby seemed so willing to accept Zack even though he acted like a pain in the rear, especially after having been turned on by someone she trusted. If she could get over all of that and still find a way to make friends and forgive people, then so could he.

"You really don't want to go through it right here, not while she's still vulnerable. Mark, come on, help me get her out of here, we still have a long way to go to get back to the elevator and we're running out of time." Milo moved forward and made to grab Ruby, but Mark stepped in between with his arms crossed against his chest. His imposing stature made Milo take a step back.

"Answer him. You're walking on very thin ice at the moment." Mark stood protectively over the girl.

"Okay, fine, but if anything happens because you're wasting time, then it's on you," Milo stammered, apparently flustered by the fact nobody would just go along with the plan in his head without further explanation.

"Well? Where would you like me to begin?" Milo asked. It was a question John wasn't ready for, one implying more secrets were being kept than those he only barely knew about. Just how tangled was this web of deceit?

"Why don't you start with what you know about

the Lavalieres in the infirmary?" Jade pulled herself up from the ground slowly, a hand pressed against the side of her head. She coughed, recoiling with a wince each time.

"Is Pavlovian trying to start an army?" John asked the question causing him the most trouble accepting.

Milo laughed, a look of absolute relief washing over his face. John couldn't understand why Milo was acting so strange, how could he find anything funny about kidnapping or hurting others? He didn't seem like he wanted to see them in trouble, at least not when he was helping rescue them from Igneous. There had to be more to the story than they knew.

"Can we at least get a move on while I straighten out your misconceptions? Even if you don't understand why, sitting here is a bad idea. Trust me." Milo's straightforward approach took John by surprise. Something about staying here was definitely worrying him. The others looked to John for guidance and he nodded his approval.

Chapter Thirteen

The others didn't trust Milo so easily, they hadn't seen what he'd done against void Igneous and didn't have John's ability to sense the truth behind his words. John made sure to keep hold of his quartz throughout their journey, scrutinizing every little thing Milo said.

Lucky for him, Mark and Riley insisted on being in charge of carrying Ruby, both of them subtly fighting over who could keep her protected better.

"Would you like some help?" John reached out to help steady Jade.

"No." She swatted his hand away and almost as an afterthought added, "Thank you."

John didn't like seeing her struggle to pull herself together, but backed off at her request. She steadied herself on the edge of the fountain and took a few deep breaths. Her process was a lot like Ruby's meditation.

"I'm always here for you if you need me. I've come to learn not everything needs to be handled alone. You can rely on your friends even if you don't think they would understand." John couldn't take his eyes off Milo as he spoke the words currently weighing on his heart.

John gave the fountain one last good look before they left the center of the labyrinth. With the water flowing again, the scene returned to one of peaceful serenity.

The demon might always be there, looming just over her shoulder and waiting for an opening, but the wolf was there to protect the girl at all times. Something about it made John feel a lot better about their situation. Even when the situation appeared bleak, he knew he could always trust in his friends to be by his side.

"I have no clue how you manage to concoct such wild theories. I told him we should have included you guys from the beginning but Pavlovian thought you wouldn't be able to handle it. Truth is, I'm not even sure if we're capable of handling the problem, and things just keep getting worse," Milo spoke cryptically, avoiding any actual details.

Every time John thought he was getting close to telling them something of worth, Milo would fall silent, picking and choosing how he would continue.

It was during one of those moments of silence John first heard a low rumble. He looked over to Mark, who was attempting not to draw attention to his stomach screaming for food. John kept his friend's dignity intact, choosing not to bring it up while they moved along the labyrinth.

Jade kept one hand lightly sweeping along the right side hedge, helping them make decisions at every fork in the path. Each decision appeared to rely on the color of the flowers they came across, and the shape of the leaves, given enough time John might have been able to figure out the patterns. He might have even enjoyed solving this logical riddle had he not been expending all his energy trying to get a straight answer out of Milo.

"You need to stop beating around the bush. What's this 'situation' you keep mentioning?" John longed for a conversation without metaphors, hyperbole, and missing information.

"Sorry, I got so used to keeping information to myself, I guess it's just a habit at this point. You know, it wasn't easy keeping this from you. Your ability to know when people are lying made it especially difficult. Honestly, I don't know how I managed to keep you thrown off this long," Milo mused, a little too proud of himself.

"You didn't, I've known you were hiding something for a long time, but I gave you the benefit of the doubt. I wanted you to feel comfortable enough to talk to me in your own time." John found himself back in the driver's seat, holding this one over Milo helped boost his confidence. He couldn't help but feel a bit smug.

"Oh, no wonder you've been so distant the past couple of days." Milo shrugged off the revelation as though it barely mattered.

"I've been distant? You're the one who kept running off in the middle of the night, turning down plans, and generally acting sketchy." John threw out the accusations, each one meant to land like a jab. He needed Milo to understand how neglected he had felt, to acknowledge his own wrongdoing.

"Not like it was my fault. Pavlovian asked me to keep quiet," Milo shot back. He wasn't doing himself any favors.

John added another tally into the "questionable" column.

"Because he's worried we wouldn't be able to handle *whatever* it is you continue to refuse to talk about." John tried to emphasize the part of the conversation he lacked.

"It's not that simple. Lavalieres are dropping unconscious. This problem is much bigger than you can even imagine. But now you have all of the facts backward, I guess it can't hurt to start sorting them out for you." Milo sighed.

Jade pulled them to the right at another fork in the path and John noticed they were passing by a set of green flowers for the second time since leaving the center. Also, the leaves took on a shape similar to those they'd passed a couple of turns previously. He glanced over to Jade, but she gave no indication of any problems. Mark's stomach continued to rumble, and by now, others were taking notice.

"When was the last time you ate?" Riley asked.

"At the diner, right?" John replied, thinking back to earlier in the day.

"Actually, didn't get the opportunity to have anything there before we had to run out," Mark reminded them.

"We'll get something when we get back." Milo promised. "According to Pavlovian the disappearances began even before Igneous attacked Gem Haven. Not many, but enough to catch the attention of the media. Your parents had a hand in that, apparently you failed to let them know you were leaving," Milo accused John. John felt a pinch in the muscles in his neck. He felt a powerful urge to lash out at Milo's insinuation this was somehow his fault.

"I did that to save you." John felt the tips of his ears grow warm.

"I know, it was only a matter of time before more reports of missing Lavalieres came in. Pavlovian was the first to notice their common connection, for the most part." Milo turned away, refusing to look John in the eyes.

"They were *precious,*" Jade replied, filling in the blank.

"Correct, there were others of course, but a vast majority of them fell into the same category. They were being targeted. The same way Igneous had targeted Lavalieres to help complete the Diadem."

"So you think whoever is doing this is trying to finish what Igneous started?" Jade paused and shook her head. The last time she encountered Igneous, he had been using Milo to help capture her. If someone was picking up where he left off, she was more than likely a target.

"We thought Zack might have been behind it. Seeing as he's Igneous' son and knew a lot more than I gave him credit for." Milo lost himself in thought for a moment.

"Zack was one of the latest victims. Just before Milo showed up to help fend off Igneous," John explained to catch the group up. "But I do know who is behind it. A girl named Felicia was the one who led us to Ruby. Her bond is with a diamond, and she can transform into a wolf, like Ruby."

"Up until now we thought the attacks were initiated by Augers. If it was known all along this was from a Lavaliere, why feed us false information?" Riley asked, latching onto something he could be angry about. John wondered if it might be the least of their issues at the moment.

"Think about it, you already proved how quick it would be to pit us against each other when lacking information. Pavlovian didn't want to risk us all turning on each other before we knew a little more about *deep sleep*." Milo looked up and stopped before following Jade down another path. John took notice as well, this time he was sure they'd passed the same grouping of flowers not too long ago.

"It didn't take me nearly this long to find the center of the labyrinth, why is it taking so long to exit?" Milo asked, glaring at Jade.

"Sorry, but I couldn't risk us walking out of here and into a trap. Right now my main concern is keeping her safe, and I couldn't be sure handing her over to you was the right choice." Jade had stalled long enough to gather all of her strength back. Even if Milo wanted to argue, he would no longer be a match for her.

"Seriously? You're putting us all in danger." As Milo said it, John heard another low grumble, except this time he knew it hadn't come from Mark's stomach. Mark fell to the ground, his head turned away from the group.

"Jeez Mark, a little bit of warning would have been nice." Riley struggled to make up for the lost support.

"Uh...guys? Just how long *has* it been since he last ate?" John asked again, this time with a completely different worry in mind. He recalled the memory Ruby shared with him, the crucial lesson she had tried to teach Felicia. All shape shifters needed to feed their gem or risk falling to their primal urges. The tiger's head turned slowly, golden eyes locked on the group.

"We have a problem." John watched his friend closely, knowing if the feral part of Mark were taking over, he'd stand absolutely no chance against his friend. The tiger's head shook, and for a moment, John wavered on whether Mark maintained control, or if the beast had taken over.

"He can't control himself. He'll hunt until he finds food." John used the temporary lapse to warn the others, but they didn't seem to get the hint until he yelled, "Run!"

Mark hunched over, ready to pounce at the first sight of movement. John silently pleaded for his friend to keep fighting. He might not know exactly what Ruby did to push herself into sequester, but he could imagine it wasn't good.

Jade pulled out her gem and whipped forth a spray of icicles. The hail was enough to catch the tiger off guard and stun him for a moment, providing just enough time for them to get a good starting lead on him.

"You've been leading us in circles, just how far away are we from the exit?" Milo yelled as they followed Jade. It was just like him to turn around and make it seem like this was somehow someone else's fault.

"The flowers follow the rainbow pattern, red at the center and purple on the outer edge," Jade replied. Armed with this information, John finally pieced together the puzzle of how she had been making a majority of her decisions whenever they reached an intersection. The bad news, they were still much closer to the center than they were the outer edge.

"Hold on, I'm not strong enough to carry Ruby by myself." Even if Riley hadn't stopped, it wouldn't have mattered. A growl from somewhere nearby meant Mark had already caught back up with them.

"Survived a major attack by Igneous just to

become a meal for Catboy..." Jade watched the corner closely, but the tiger didn't appear. John continued to listen and heard the low growling, following it up to the side of a hedge, where he pinpointed the source.

"He's on the other side...how long do you think it would take him to figure out how to get around?" John asked, but nobody wanted to come up with an answer.

"We're no match for a hunting animal. Maybe it isn't about getting around it..." Riley started but John had to jump in.

"Him, not *it*," John replied, cringing at Riley's ability to reduce his friend down to nothing more than an animal.

"Him," Riley corrected himself, "Maybe we've been going about this the wrong way, the hotel will keep us safe if we die..." He couldn't seem able to bring himself to finish the statement.

"No, even if we all regenerate somewhere else in the hotel, Pavlovian thinks the process would separate her mind from her body. It's too risky," Milo explained, pulling the option off the table.

There was a momentary silence from the other side of the hedge, and then the entire wall shook, the branches on the other side making loud rustling noises as the tiger apparently leapt into it. John stumbled to the side, his heart lodged in his throat. Another growl followed by another wall-shaking leap.

"He's following you, John." Jade and the others were just as close to the hedge as he was, but a couple of feet away from him. She was right. Every time he moved, Mark matched his pace on the other side. John reached into his pocket and pulled out the catnip-filled toy. He'd completely forgotten about it. He'd only picked it up as a joke.

A mighty roar came from the other side of the hedge. Pulling out the toy must have increased the potency reaching the tiger. Mark slammed into the hedge, shaking the leaves, as though he were trying to break through.

"You've been leading him to us this entire time," Riley yelled, throwing his hands into the air. John lowered his head, and his shoulders sagged. If it hadn't been for him, they may have been able to make it back to the entrance.

"Wait, he's following the catnip. We could use it to buy us the time we need." John ripped open the rat, which threw the tiger into even more of a frenzy.

Chapter Fourteen

"How can we know for sure he'll go after the catnip rather than us?" John asked while holding the headless rat clamped shut.

"We can't just leave the catnip here and hope he goes after it. If one of us stayed behind, it would give the others a chance to escape," Milo said, looking around the group as though he wanted someone to volunteer.

"Sounds like the kind of thing Mark would suggest."

John saw the problem immediately. Jade was necessary to help lead the others out of the maze, Riley because he was now the only one strong enough to carry Ruby, and nobody trusted Milo enough to leave him on his own.

"I'll do it," John volunteered. A twitch coursed through the back of his neck as he understood what he was volunteering for. A sense of calm washed over him. He knew he could do this.

"No, I can't let you...you can't." Milo's tough guy act began to falter. His eyes betrayed him more than anything else. Those soft brown eyes, kind and caring.

John had seen this look from him before, the first time he'd seen him again just after defeating Igneous. No matter what secrets Milo might have been keeping, he couldn't hide his genuine feelings from John.

"It has to be me," John logically explained the conclusion he'd reached.

Milo shook his head, blinking a few too many times, a technique John had used in the past to hide any signs of an emotional response.

"We'll figure out another way," he said after a moment, his voice just barely holding steady.

"What if we freeze it?" Jade asked and John's shoulders sagged. She still didn't seem to understand Mark was still a person.

"He. Not it," John replied shortly. "And we already tried. We aren't fast enough to freeze him and get away."

"No, I mean *it*, the catnip." Jade pointed to the rat in John's fist, his tight grip on the plush toy had turned his knuckles white. John couldn't quite follow where she was going with her suggestion.

"We spread a little at each junction and freeze it, keep him thrown off track and buy more time." Jade beamed.

"Not a bad idea," Milo conceded.

John pulled some catnip from the toy. The smell was a lot stronger, and he expected Mark to get thrown into a frenzy. Instead, there was complete silence from the other side of the hedge. He shared a confused glance with the others. Out of the corner of his eye, an orange streak leapt out from behind a corner. John's knees locked in place, too frightened to move. Within moments the cat was upon him, he fell backward, a bunch of the catnip spilled out onto him.

Instead of tearing out his jugular, a distinct possibility running through John's head, the cat stopped and sniffed at the air. He lowered his head and clawed at the ground, tilling clumps of dirt and grass.

John's heart dropped when the tiger looked back at him, a new hunger in his eyes. There was a feral quality in the beast's stance. He knew John was the source of the catnip.

Without thinking, John gathered up a bunch of the catnip and threw it over Mark's head.

Mark growled, following his treat. He jumped away from the group in pursuit of the intoxicating substance. They didn't need to think twice. John forced himself to turn his back on the tiger, running with the others. The last thing he saw before they turned a corner was Mark rolling around on the ground, one paw constantly swiping at a single spot on the hedge wall.

"How much do you have left?" Jade asked as they rushed around another corner, the flowers changing color to indicate they had made it another step closer to the exit. John pulled out the floppy rat toy and peered into the opening. Quite a bit had spilled out already.

"A little less than half," John said.

"We'll have to use it sparingly, but here might be a good spot." Jade pointed to the opposite path.

John pulled some out and threw it down the wrong path.

"No, more," Jade said as she pulled out her gem.

John worried it wouldn't be enough, especially if she was going to cover the scent. John hoped Mark would choose to follow the scent of the catnip rather than them. The only good news was that there was no sign yet he had begun tracking them again.

They pressed on, spreading a bit of catnip and then layering it with a thin sheet of ice on top.

They did this at multiple junctions, and as the

flowers began to bloom red, John was down to the last little bit remaining. Riley and Milo carefully propped Ruby up against the side of the hedge. Both failing to conceal their own fatigue.

Jade led John over to the intersection. John tipped over the plush toy and shook out the last of the contents. This was it. Hopefully, they were close enough to the elevator it wouldn't matter. John dug into the toy and scraped out as much of the catnip as he could, but there wasn't much.

They hadn't heard Mark in quite some time, but it didn't alleviate their worry. Tigers were known for silently hunting their prey. Jade was just putting on her finishing touches when they heard a guttural growl.

John looked up, expecting to see they had been overtaken by Mark's hunting skills. But the sound hadn't come from him. The four of them turned to see the glow of the wolf's eyes staring back at them.

"Ruby, you're awake." Riley ran over, dropped to his knees, and threw his arms around the wolf.

John was forced to disregard his natural urge to run away from such an imposing predator. Instead, he carefully approached the animal, remembering it was the same girl he'd met before. But why was she taking the form of the wolf?

"What? How is this possible?" Milo looked over the wolf, his face contorted into confused curiosity.

"She woke up. Does it really matter why?" Riley asked, clearly annoyed by Milo's lack of sympathy.

"Of all the Lavalieres who came in unconscious, she's the only one to wake up. Don't you find that a bit strange?" Milo asked, keeping a wary eye on the wolf before them. John found himself conflicted. On the one hand, the two of them were able to come back from the nightmare realm before. Ruby was also very resourceful and quick on the uptake, maybe she had seen how they did it, and copied them. On the other hand, it was a bit strange for her to suddenly wake up and shift into wolf form. When the wolf looked into John's eyes, he could see a softening in her cheek fur.

"You just woke up, it's okay. Can you change back?" John asked. The wolf reared her head back and let out a mighty howl. The echo reverberated through the maze. It sounded different, off in some way from the one he remembered.

"Stop," Jade yelled, startling Ruby. "We have another anthro Lavaliere chasing after us. You're going to give away our position."

As if on cue, the tiger leapt from the opposite side, trapping the group between the two beasts. John was out of time, out of catnip, and definitely out of ideas. Mark roared in triumph, not even giving a second glance in the direction of the last trap they had set. They were out of luck.

John's memory flashed back to the moment he first died. Standing there in the middle of a war zone, just a game to the residents of Gem Haven, a sick and twisted game pitting friends against each other in a deadly version of capture the flag, John had been thrown into it the moment he stepped foot inside the hotel as though his death was destined.

Jade had been the one who killed him the first time. Her cold icicle penetrated his heart just after he embraced Milo. First there was pain, but then...nothing. The hotel brought him back to life, like a reset button. But in those few moments of death, there had been peace.

Even knowing how little death meant in the hotel didn't ease his mind. He looked into the eyes of his friend, ready to accept his fate. He knew Mark was still in there, but not enough to control himself. John took a step forward, squaring off with the tiger. He was ready.

"Sit." The command came from a voice he hadn't truly heard until that moment. A voice he hadn't expected. Mark fell to the ground, knees bent in submission. John turned to see his savior, Ruby, standing tall in her human form.

"How did you do that?" Jade asked.

"There's a pecking order among anthros, someone higher up on the chain can give orders to those beneath them." Ruby's voice was both calm and calculated. The smile she wore seemed foreign and distant.

"It's true." John remembered how it felt when Felicia had given orders to Ruby. Even though it was just him seeing her memory, he could still feel the absolute need to obey her orders. It sent shivers up his spine. And now Ruby was exerting her commands on Mark. But one thing nagged at him. She, of all people, knew what it was like to have someone force her to do something. How could she turn around and do it to someone else?

"Where are we?" Ruby asked.

"We brought you to Gem Haven. We're in Jade's labyrinth. Are you okay?" While Riley was busy checking on Ruby, John kept his eyes on his friend. Mark continued growling, but didn't move from his spot. It was surreal. John could see him struggling to disobey the orders.

"We should wake the others," Ruby suggested.

Jade appeared hesitant to leave Mark, but ultimately turned away from the beast and inched toward the final leg of the maze.

John wasn't sure he felt comfortable leaving his friend behind. It was one thing when they were being chased but now Mark seemed helpless. It didn't seem right. Ruby continued as if it was no big deal to leave him behind.

John brought up the rear, watching as Ruby clung tight to Jade's heels. She ignored Riley's attempts to engage in conversation. John was an only child, but even he could see their familial bond looked a bit one sided. Jade paused at the next junction, and Ruby stumbled into her. A twig snapped beneath her feet. The sound penetrated his ears. He knew Ruby was too careful to accidentally make that sound.

"You're not Ruby."

Everything seemed so clear to him now. This wasn't the kind-hearted girl he'd met in the dream world. He realized his outburst might have been a bit premature when everyone turned to him. Each of them stared with a confused look about them, except Ruby. Her narrowed eyes and stern frown gave him the impression she was less than happy with him calling her out.

"Who are you?" he asked her, his hand hovering automatically around his quartz. Having not yet sensed any outright lies from her, he was wary and careful about with how he phrased the question.

"My name is Ruby. I was put to sleep by another Lavaliere. All I want to do is help the others." With each major lie coming from Ruby's lips, John felt the acid burn and bubble up from the back of his throat.

Sharp pains rose from his chest. It made him want to puke. Her lies weren't harmless like Mark's. They were malicious.

"John, are you okay?" Jade asked.

He doubled over, spitting on the ground in a meager attempt to dispel her deceit. He wanted to warn them, tell them not to trust a single thing this girl was saying. But he fumbled over the words. They were like a flood trying to push up and over a dam. He grew frustrated as the waters welled even higher. He knew the only way he would be able to get the information across would be if he calmed down. He needed to open the gates.

"He's not looking so good." She deflected the focus of the conversation away from herself, another technique to avoid being exposed in her lie.

The way she carried herself was beginning to irk John. There was only one person he knew with her demeanor and ability to sway people with words. It was too much, and finally a tiny trickle of water poured up and over the dam.

"Felicia."

Chapter Fifteen

John's quartz pulsed in his fist. Power coursed through him as he unraveled Felicia's lies. She may have taken Ruby's body, but the girl was every pound for pound as manipulative as a sleazy used car salesman.

"Admit it, you're not Ruby." John took a step forward, closing the gap between them.

Her features relaxed, the edge of her mouth curled into a slight smile. He liked it better when she looked angry. This girl knew just how to toy with every emotion. Her deceiving innocence was disarming.

"Why would you think such a thing? Do you have any idea what it's like to be trapped inside your own head?" Felicia stood her ground. John frowned, replaying what she'd said as if he was listening to a tape on loop. She avoided the lie. In doing so, she stripped him of his power.

"What have you done with my sister?" Riley stepped forward.

"You don't actually believe him, do you?" Felicia ran a finger along her forehead, tucking strands of red hair behind her ear.

"Of course we do." Jade came from behind and placed both hands on the sides of Ruby's head. Felicia gasped, her hands flying to meet Jade's. Before she could wrench them off, the whites of her eyes turned

121

blue and she slumped down to the ground.

Riley shoved Jade aside.

"What did you do to her?" He knelt down next to his sister's body. Jade recovered, but didn't retaliate.

"She's not your sister. John said it was a disguise, and John can't lie." Jade gathered her composure and pushed off the blame of the results of her action on him. Personally, he was glad she stepped up, but he wasn't happy he'd have to correct her.

"To clarify, I'm not sure how she did it, but this is Ruby's body. Felicia is controlling her." He couldn't let them turn her brain into a popsicle over a small misunderstanding. John's words came back to him now, no longer under the stress of having to react to an immediate threat.

"She's still breathing," Riley confirmed.

"Then what should we do with her?" Jade asked, hands firmly pressed against her hips.

"I think we should continue on as planned. We can get her back to Pavlovian and figure out what to do from there." Milo's suggestion stirred the momentum of the group.

John's heart was still racing, but he managed to keep calm, at least on the surface. While Riley and Milo picked up the unconscious Ruby, John avoided making eye contact, guilty over his inability to help the group in any special way. It should have been him getting left behind in the labyrinth instead of Mark.

"You said we had to hurry. Did you know something about this?" Jade asked as she led the group on.

"This wasn't quite what we were expecting. There's a common link between all of the sleepers—"

"They're all precious gem users," Jade offered.

"Actually, no. After running some tests on the first few, Pavlovian noticed they were overproducing some kind of chemical which induces sleep. The machines he has them hooked up to are keeping that chemical balanced."

"Are we sure that's safe?" Jade stopped suddenly, and John took notice of the red flowers surrounding them. They were almost free of the maze.

"It's safer than not doing anything. Pavlovian says if they continue to overproduce, it will have lasting negative effects on them when they wake up," Milo said.

"If they wake up," Jade corrected him.

"Put me down," the voice was Ruby's, but the command was Felicia's. Riley immediately set her down, but when Milo faltered, she toppled uneasily to her knees. Jade was quick to react, whipping out her gem and preparing to strike with another icy blow.

"No, don't hurt her." Riley held the ground between his sister and his friend.

"She's dangerous," Jade replied.

"We don't know for sure." The two of them tussled, affording Felicia the opportunity to regain her composure. She slowly brought herself up and cringed.

"What did you do to me?" Felicia's hands pressed up against the sides of her head, and her eyes clenched shut.

Milo reached for his necklace, but John shook his head. He was beginning to understand, acting first and asking questions later was the reason they were in this predicament in the first place. His powers relied on knowledge, and he had spent far too long in the dark.

All this time he'd been envious of the others. He wished he had the raw power and force that came with controlling ice like Jade. Or the ability to manipulate his physical form like Mark. Or being there as comfort and protection, healing those who were hurt like Lily. He even built up Milo, assuming the necklace he wore meant he had new and potentially amazing powers. A conclusion he'd jumped to faster than a bolt of lightning travels from sky to ground.

All of this, he realized, was due to his own insecurities. He considered his power to be little more than a simple parlor trick. His ability to decipher between lies and the truth…he couldn't see how it would possibly be useful in any meaningful way. Even his short glimpses of the future seemed meaningless without the capability of diverting or redirecting its path.

But he could see now that without it he'd have never met Milo. He never would have had a meaningful bond with Mark. And most importantly, he never would have been able to warn them about Felicia. He needed to stop doubting his own abilities and start utilizing them. He was the only one of the group who could get her to talk and tell them the truth.

"What have you done with Ruby?" John asked her directly. He stepped forward, no longer afraid of this girl.

"Like I said before, I am Ruby," she insisted, but the bad taste left in his mouth told a different story. He refocused and pushed the power of the lie back through his quartz.

"We know you're lying. *Tell us what you are doing here*." He flourished his words, mixing them together with the strength of his gem.

"I'm here to claim the Diadem and destroy Pavlovian." She clamped a hand down over her mouth, eyes growing wide. "How did you...? Nobody should be able to command me." Her scowl grew furious.

Now he had her on the ropes. He had the upper hand. She could no longer deny her plans without empowering him.

"Better think twice before lying to John," Jade taunted Felicia.

"What did you do with Ruby?" John asked, his confidence growing with every passing moment.

And then she smiled, causing John to pause. He expected her to lie to him again. He expected he would turn around and correct her. And he expected he once again would use his power to force an answer out of her. But there was one thing he hadn't accounted for.

"This was supposed to be easy. I'm beginning to understand why Zack failed in his attempts to infiltrate Gem Haven. You're all so sheltered in here that you don't even realize there's a war going on. A war Pavlovian started and Igneous will end," Felicia said. Her words felt calculated as though she were carefully treading a minefield in order to avoid triggering John's manipulation.

"Got some bad news for you and your crusade. You're too late. Igneous is gone. We defeated him." Jade broke away from Riley's hold.

"You did manage to make things difficult, but that's what also makes it fun, don't you think? You see, it's not simple to destroy an idea once it has taken root. You would know better than anyone, wouldn't you, Milo?" Felicia said.

"What do you mean?" Milo appeared caught off guard.

"Like a fire, it might start off small enough, but it will grow and it will spread beyond your control." Felicia sounded like she was egging him on, but something clicked, and John began to understand what she was saying. She was still talking about Igneous. Not his ideas or beliefs, but the idea of him. She was trying to bring him back.

"One way or another, we will complete the Diadem," Felicia said.

"We can't allow you to do that." Milo reached for his necklace and pulled out a smooth bright green piece of malachite.

"I was really hoping we could do this the easy way. *Sleep.*" Felicia issued the command.

The word echoed in John's head. He tried to maintain his focus, to keep himself anchored to the hotel, to the labyrinth. He was failing.

"Won't work on me." Milo's voice seemed distant.

John's eyelids grew heavy, and his knees threatened to give way. John clamped his teeth down on his tongue, a trick he used in class whenever his teachers got too boring. It wasn't enough to counteract the effects washing over him.

"Good to know, but who says I was aiming for you?" These were the last words he heard from Felicia as the sandman claimed his resolve. The last thing he saw was Milo turning to face him. And the last thing he felt was Milo catching him as he fell back into the nightmare realm.

A void shadow flit across his field of view. As he watched, it darted away and off into the distance.

Flashes of light flickered from an unknown source. *No.* He pinched his arm and tried everything he could to wake himself up.

"John, thank goodness, you're back. We have a problem," Abby called out to him.

He whipped around, feeling wide-awake inside this dream. Being thrown into another bad situation was the last thing on his mind. He desperately wanted to get back to the labyrinth to help his friends take on Felicia. It wasn't until he got a good long look at the group that he realized no matter how bad things were in the real world, he couldn't just leave these guys to fend for themselves here in the nightmare realm.

"Where's Ruby?" John asked, after scanning the entire group and finding no sign of her. In fact, there seemed to be a couple of others missing as well. Abby chewed on her lip ring, her eyes lowering.

"You mean she didn't wake up? She disappeared suddenly. We assumed she was back with you."

Abby's words chilled him. John tried to ignore the shadows flitting around them as he explained what was happening back in the labyrinth. By the time he was finished, there was only one person in the group not whispering among the others. Zack. He stood in the back of the group. While the others reacted to his story with mild curiosity, Zack appeared to be muttering angrily.

John was surprised to see him still sticking around, considering Ruby was the leader who managed to keep him with the group in the first place. And then he remembered, Felicia had mentioned a Zack, could it have been the same guy?

"You…you tried to infiltrate Gem Haven. Are you

working with Felicia?" John pointed out Zack and everyone fell silent.

"Ruby!" Abby broke off from the group, sprinting in the opposite direction of the shadows' movement, dodging them as she went. John didn't think twice, he abandoned his confrontation with Zack, speaking with Ruby was much more important.

"I...I couldn't speak. I couldn't move." Tears streamed down Ruby's cheeks. She looked up at John and choked out the words, "I'm sorry."

He held out a hand and helped her up off the ground. Immediately the three of them found themselves in the center of one of the biggest group hugs ever.

"What happened?" John managed to ask once his lungs were no longer being crushed by everyone. This was the kind of friendship and comradery he loved to see. The emotions were pure and real, even though the only thing connecting each of them was this shared dream.

"I woke up. I couldn't believe it. But when I tried to move, I couldn't. I tried to scream but I couldn't. All I could do was watch as Felicia controlled me. I was paralyzed. It was the most frightening thing ever."

Ruby closed her eyes and shuddered. A shiver crawled down John's spine. Her recollection was one he empathized with far too well. When he was a kid, he used to wake up in the middle of his dreams unable to move his body, a condition called sleep paralysis. He'd never wish it on his worst enemies.

Chapter Sixteen

All John wanted to do was curl up in a nice warm bed and fall asleep. If only he could wake up with all of his problems solved and everything returned to normal. He was stuck between two worlds.

Milo might have shown up to help with Igneous, but it was John who'd stuck around long enough to gain Ruby's trust. In the eyes of those who had been forced here by Felicia, he was the master of this world.

He couldn't sit back any longer and watch this movie play out with him in the audience. He had to step up and lead. He might not be able to stop Felicia from here, but the two worlds were much more connected than they might seem.

"Can anyone tell me anything about these shadows?" He needed to understand what was going on here. If he could, he might be able to find a way back. The problem started with Felicia, but he got the feeling that the shadows held the answers. Sleepers became lucid whenever their personal demons were defeated. At the very least, it would be a good place to start.

"The shadows seem to be gaining in strength, all heading in that direction. We were about to follow them when we were attacked by Felicia."

"We need to follow them and find out what's happening." A fire awakened within him. Felicia may have forced him to sleep, but by no means did he have to hibernate.

"This started up after you left," Abby explained. "We think it has something to do with Zack's father, Igneous, but the only way to know for sure is to follow them."

"You'll never stand a chance against my father. Not even if you managed to figure out what you're missing." Zack raised his head, locking a menacing gaze on John. A lopsided sneer proved Ruby never should have put any trust in this guy.

Zack charged at John with blinding speed. His feet blurred as they barely tapped the ground.

John raised his arm, beckoning shadows to form around him in the shape of a shield, but he was too slow.

Zack dove at John, arms outstretched. John expected to get knocked backward by the blow, but instead Zack went *into* him, disappearing into his chest as the two made contact. A searing pain tore through John's body, as though Zack was ripping him in half from the inside. John collapsed to the ground, clawing at his chest as if digging out the rooted parasite would alleviate his pain. His head exploded in a fireball of a migraine.

The group gathered around him, and he could see their lips moving, but couldn't hear what they were saying. Ruby pushed her way to the front of the group, leaning down next to him. He tried to keep his eyes focused on her, on what she was saying, but another wave of pain washed over him. He clenched his eyes shut, depriving himself of the last of his senses.

As he lay in total darkness, voices began to seep through the cracks. The searing pain in his head dulled to a low roar, and his body eventually relaxed.

"What did you do to him? I'll kill you," Milo yelled.

The voice John heard was distant and echoing, as though it was there and also somewhere far away. Another shot of pain swept through John as his eyes were forced open.

Through the mists of the dream world, he could make out a hazy view of the labyrinth.

"Killing me wouldn't be of any use, I'd just go back to my own body, and Ruby would be dead. I'm sure you wouldn't want that. Now step aside." Felicia pushed Milo out of the way.

John tried to push himself up off the ground, but his arms wouldn't move. He tried to control his legs, but they were like stone. He strained to move any part of his body, but even though his mind was active, his body was paralyzed. He silently screamed.

"Wow, this is cool." John felt his mouth moving, felt the vibrato in his throat, and heard the words said in his voice. But he wasn't in the driver's seat.

"I told you I could get us in Gem Haven, Zack." Felicia reached out a hand and pulled John to his feet.

"No!" Both he and Milo screamed in unison, although only one could be heard. John struggled, pushing against the intruder Zack, who'd taken control of his body. He needed to get control back. His body had to obey his command, but John couldn't even clench his fist or wiggle his toes at his command...or for that matter, anything else.

Another thought occurred to him as he continued to fight for control. Being paralyzed and at the mercy of someone else meant he was completely trapped. As this realization washed over him, phantom aches and pains spread out through his body. The only reason he knew they weren't real was because Zack hadn't reacted to them. John felt physically and mentally exhausted. He would have collapsed if he was capable.

"*Report,*" Felicia commanded, and John felt obligated to reply.

Although when his mouth opened, it was Zack responding. "They are beginning to figure out how the shadows are serving to reform Igneous. He is nearly ready for transferal. The Dreamcatcher is back in the nightmare realm." Zack's words came from John seamlessly. Although John hadn't completely understood much of what was said, he knew none of it could have been any good.

"Can you hear me, John?" Ruby's ghostly distant voice rang out. He concentrated and heard other voices picking up around him. As they became clearer, the world around him melted down, the labyrinth walls fell and splashed into the abyss of the void. The world of the hotel collapsed around him. His friends were the last to disappear into the mists of the nightmare realm.

He could move again, he blinked and clenched his fists. It was a wonderful feeling. He breathed a heavy sigh of relief and began chuckling uncontrollably. It felt so good to be in control again, even if it meant being stuck back in the nightmare realm.

"John, we saw everything. It was like you projected the images around us. I've never seen anything like it here before," Abby said as the last remaining pieces of the labyrinth disappeared around them.

"I couldn't move. I couldn't speak." John knew he

must sound crazy, but he didn't care. It had been possibly the most terrifying few minutes of his life.

Ruby just nodded in understanding. She had gone through the same thing. "It was awkward being trapped as she used me like a puppet," Ruby said.

"It was helpful," Abby mused. She was positively bouncing with excitement.

"How so?" John asked, his body shaking for an entirely different reason. He never wanted to feel so restricted again in his life.

"It gives us some insight into their plans. Now we know for sure they are trying to bring Igneous back. Even better, we know they can't do it, yet. And best of all, we know how to stop them." Abby beamed.

"We do?" John asked. They were nearly destroyed last time they faced Igneous, and they may not have even beaten him then if Milo hadn't shown up.

"It sounds like the Dreamcatcher is what we need to stop Igneous."

"How will we find it?" John asked.

"I can do more than just locate people." Abby held up her necklace with a smile.

"We don't really know for sure though. Searching might be a waste of time. We should go directly after Igneous to stop him from forming," Ruby said and tugged on John's arm.

John was torn between the two. On one hand, they were limited on time and didn't know for sure this Dreamcatcher could be used as a weapon against Igneous. On the other hand, if there was something they could use to sway a battle in their favor, they should make every attempt at locating such an item.

"I'm sorry, Ruby, but I think we need to find the

Dreamcatcher before we go after Igneous. Abby, please proceed." John made his decision.

"I'm getting something." A bubble appeared in front of them, floating away from the group. With little time to think, they gave chase.

"Look, there." Abby picked up her pace as the orb slowed a short distance away. Wisps of shadow ebbed around them, billowing up from the ground. The closer they got, the harder it was to see their feet as the fog thickened.

The shadows stopped moving and pulled together, reforming around the group. Twisted and mangled trees reached from the ground. The visuals created around them out of the shadows were more vivid and detailed than he had seen before. He could even hear an eerie whistling of wind through the trees as they stepped into an overgrown cemetery.

"We entered a *nightmare*." Ruby tread forth with caution.

Shadows arched up out of the ground, taking shape as rough chiseled gravestones. John knelt beside the closest one and read the effigy.

Rose Flower
Beloved Grandmother

The ground below John trembled and softened beneath his knees. The dirt gave away and the grave opened up to swallow him. He screamed and reached out to find something to grasp onto. He clawed at the dirt, but it crumbled and collapsed under his fingernails. His feet dangled over the side as he slipped farther and farther into the grave.

Abby's hand grabbed his, stopping his descent just as his body slammed up against the wall. He turned his head to keep from getting a face full of mud.

John kicked and felt the wall give way just enough to create a makeshift step. With Abby's help, he managed to climb free, crawling up and over the edge. Once he was sure he was far enough away to keep from being buried alive again, he spat and wiped away the dirt around his mouth with the back of his wrist.

He wasn't the only one who'd fallen into trouble though. Around him, others dealt with trees whose branches had taken on a life of their own. The mangled limbs wrapped around his friends, restraining them as they struggled to fight back against the demonic timber.

"John, you and Abby find the Dreamcatcher. I'll help them." Ruby split off and doubled back to help the others.

Thickening fog separated them from rest of the group. A faint beacon of light glowed just beyond a patch of mist in front of them. John and Abby hurried to catch up with the light as it led them deeper into the nightmare. When they approached an overgrown mausoleum, with ivy climbing up the crumbling brick walls, the orb stopped in front of the arched entrance. A rusty barred door guarded the objects within.

"Why must graveyards always have a creep factor?" John joked, but it didn't help alleviate the tension. An overwhelming sense of dread wrapped its icy grip around him.

"It's in there. Are you ready?" Abby's resolve impressed him. But even the strength of conviction in her voice was negated when she remained frozen in place. John nodded and reached for the handle. The cold metal practically froze the palm of his hand. He pulled open the door with a creak, and a bell rang once.

John and Abby shared a momentary look of confusion, but made their way inside.

In the center of the room, a stone coffin was positioned on a raised dais. With the light of the orb, John was able to make out multiple effigies located throughout the hollowed out room. Along the walls, stone tablets carried names and dates, as well as short sentences of remembrance.

What creeped out John the most wasn't so much what these slabs represented, but rather who they were designated for. Milo, Mark, and Jayden. *Jayden?* He didn't dwell on it for long, as one final grave chilled him to the bone. His own name was chiseled into the stone tablet.

They made their way to the center and stood over the tomb. One name was missing, the sleeper he knew they would find inside.

"Help me open the casket." John planted his feet firmly on the ground and pushed against the concrete slab. At first, it refused to budge, but as they worked together and combined their strength, it slowly opened to reveal the sleeper inside.

Lily gasped for breath, her eyes closed tightly.

"Lily, can you hear me? You need to wake up." Abby reached out to her, and as she got closer, the building around them began to shake and tremble.

"Not going to work, we need to make her feel safe." John remembered the ringing bell and knew exactly what he needed to do. "Wait here."

He ran back outside. There was more than enough space just above the entrance. He hoped Lily's subconscious would recognize a drastic change imprinted on her dream. He focused his thoughts on a single crystal clear image, a decorative star adorning the mausoleum. As he pictured it, the building shifted and bent to his will. Shadows converged over the exterior wall, solidifying to form a decorative star.

He ran back inside.

The choking noises ceased, replaced by a single sharp intake of breath as Lily sat up inside the coffin.

"Where am I? Abby? John? Is that you?" Lily asked, but even as she took in her surroundings, the shadowed constructs were already falling apart as her nightmare dissipated. The mausoleum walls disappeared and the mists rolled away.

John felt new life surge through him. No matter how trapped they were, he knew they would get through it.

"Welcome to our nightmare." John helped her out of the coffin. John took a deep breath, allowing himself to feel at ease. The only thing left to do was confront Igneous.

Chapter Seventeen

"Isn't a dreamcatcher one of those decorative ornaments you hang in your bedroom window? The kind that look like a spider web." John scratched his head. His entire world view had flipped too many times recently for him to keep count.

"Short answer, yes, but a dreamcatcher is much more than a simple ornament. They were woven and hung in the rooms of children. The design was symbolic, meant to entrap nightmares while allowing peaceful dreams to go through," Ruby explained.

"And you think I'm *the* Dreamcatcher?" Lily asked, her voice more whimsical than usual.

John couldn't quite put his finger on it, but there was a difference between her and the rest of them.

"We were searching for it and my power led us right to you," Abby explained.

"There's dark energy forming. I can feel it." Lily looked out toward where the shadows were gathering.

John sensed the darkness, too. Igneous had gained strength and seemed to be pulling everything in the dream world to him like a giant magnet.

"They're trying to bring Igneous back." John filled Lily in on Felicia's plans. Every fiber of his being buzzed with a tinge of electricity. The hairs on his arm stood on end as a steady pulse picked up. Igneous was growing stronger. He wished he knew how his friends were faring with Felicia.

"So Lily, if you are the Dreamcatcher, the only thing left is to stop him. What's the plan?" Abby crossed her arms; her slight hint of a smile gave off a vibe of confidence and accomplishment.

"I don't know. What exactly am I supposed to do when we get there?" Lily asked but the returned silence spoke volumes. The ground below them hummed and shifted. What remained of the graveyard dirt solidified into brick and illuminated a golden yellow in color.

"Seriously? We might as well follow it." John led the others as they set out down the path.

Off in the distance, the mists had grown into a shade of ominous emerald green. He half expected a tornado to come out of nowhere and sweep them all away. Abby tugged at his arm and pulled him off to the side.

"Lily's actually asleep. She's not under Felicia's influence. If we aren't careful there's a chance she might wake up." Abby kept her voice low and pointed out the realism in the details around them. John had to admit it was as if they were walking through another sleeper's nightmare. The colors and details down to the tiniest cracks in the bricks were vivid enough to be discernable.

"Where did she go?" Abby yelled out, and for a moment, John panicked, wondering if Lily had woken up from her fragile sleep state. But she was still walking along almost half dazed at the front of the pack.

"She was right there a second ago." Ruby pointed to an empty spot. One of the girls, the one bonded with a ruby, was nowhere to be found.

"She woke up?" Abby's tone came with a hint of sadness, but if she was right, it could only be a good thing. It meant Milo and the others might have found a way to stop Felicia. One by one, the others disappeared from the dream world. As their numbers dwindled, John's heart leapt in his chest. They were getting closer to Igneous, and all this time he'd hoped they would be able to rely on the advantage of numbers. But he was powerless to halt the process.

Soon only the four of them remained. Ruby, Abby, Lily, and himself. John was able to see the connection immediately. They were the ones not currently under Pavlovian's watch. Lily was still in her bed at the hotel. Ruby's body was still under Felicia's control. Abby didn't know where she was, or she was refusing to say. And he was Zack's puppet.

"We can't let this slow us down. Igneous must be stopped." John's announcement brought a new confidence to the diminished group. The four continued down the yellow brick road.

There was no whimsical city at the end of their journey, no castle made of sparkling gems, and nobody claiming they could grant their hearts' desires. Instead, as they approached the pulsating mists of shadow, all John could feel was a constant dread.

He couldn't bring himself to take another step. Every ounce of his being wanted to turn around and run away, to find a way to wake up from this nightmare. He wondered if Lily had any actual clue what they were getting themselves into. It was possible she was going through this as if it were any other dream. But when he studied the way she carried herself, he knew the truth. Waking her up in the graveyard had given her enough lucidity to process fully what they were doing.

Through his friend's resolve, he knew he could pull himself together and take on Igneous. The major difference, this time around, was that he couldn't rely on Milo coming to bail him out.

Abby and Ruby had their hands interlocked behind their backs. John felt his heart drop to the pit of his stomach. He hadn't even realized they had begun to meditate. It was like showing up to a class five minutes before and finding out you have a major exam you hadn't studied for. Instead of admitting he wasn't prepared, he crossed his arms behind his back.

John led the group into battle, making their way to the very end of the yellow brick road. The pathway stopped short with mists and shadows dancing circles around them.

"If you think you can stop me, you're already too late." A powerful voice boomed out, accompanied by flashes of light. The four of them huddled together, backs to each other as they looked out amongst the storm. The terrible voice had come from everywhere and nowhere at once.

"Show yourself, you coward," Abby yelled into the mist.

The shadows converged, pulling together to give form to an oversized cloaked head floating in the air around them. John felt tiny under the powerful glare of Igneous' glowing eyes. He shrunk back, attempting to avoid locking eyes with the monster, but there was nowhere to hide.

"The fog is too thick. I can't figure out where he is." Abby sent out an orb of light that quickly disappeared into the mists, swallowed up by the surrounding darkness.

"I know what makes fog disappear." Lily tilted her head toward the sky and held her hands out to her sides. It started off slow, only a couple drops at first but soon the pattering rain on the ground turned into drums as a heavy downpour swept through.

John shielded his eyes just enough to keep the rain out of them, and watched as the shadows receded and the fog escaped.

The floating mist of Igneous' form disappeared. Laughing behind the curtain of rain was a solid figure of a man in a cloak. Just behind him stood a tall pillar of black void rising high above their heads. At the base was a small crack, with light streaming through. John's hand instinctively reached for his gem, but it wasn't around his neck.

Igneous raised his sword and funneled more void through his body into the hilt, sucking it in like it was an energy source. Before John could react, Igneous swung, releasing a torrent of void.

John imagined a shield in front of him, a wall to block the sword's attack like the one Jade had raised when he tried to protect her. The shield rose a moment too late, and the powerful void slammed into John, sending him flying backward through the air.

John landed on the ground with a thud and waited for the pain that never coursed through his body. The dull phantom memory of pain served as a reminder that no matter how real any of this felt, it was still just a dream.

"I will escape. You cannot stop me." Igneous turned and swung his sword at the tower, focusing a torrential blast at the pillar. Pieces of the tower broke off, and a burst of light flooded the area. When it subsided, the crack had grown larger.

Ruby was on her feet in an instant, charging at the monster.

Igneous turned and snatched her arm, picked her up like she was a ragdoll, and tossed her to the ground. John pulled himself to his feet as Igneous loomed over his friend. Lightning sparked out from the crack in the pillar, and Ruby tried to pick herself up. Igneous' foot slammed into her chest, and a resounding crack echoed as it connected. Ruby flipped around and fell on her back.

An icy chill washed over John as Igneous raised his arms. Everything felt as if it was occurring in slow motion.

The shadows drew up into Igneous. A ball of void swirled between the monster's hands. He was going to kill her.

John clenched his fists, imagining he was tearing the ground apart. In his gut, he felt the world separate, shadows bursting forth to do his bidding. He rose into the air. His body, weightless yet completely under his control, flew forward, propelled by the shadows under his command.

Igneous failed to see John barreling toward him. The shadow ball above his head had grown massive. Ruby's scream pierced the dream world as the explosive energy crashed down over her.

John collided with the monster, sending him crashing into the black pillar as another flash of light flooded the area. But he'd flown too far past the pillar. He corrected himself and turned around, hovering in midair. A small crater covered in scorch marks remained at the empty spot where Ruby had been pinned to the ground. There was no sign of her. He'd been too late. John had failed. His blood boiled.

"No," John screamed. Igneous had killed her.

John didn't want to believe that it was true. He dove at the cloaked figure like a falcon swooping in to pick off a bit of prey. His hands morphed into talons and ripped into the fabric as he snatched Igneous from the ground and slammed him against the pillar.

His actions were automatic and wild, being directed solely from his subconscious. He lashed out with the power of the dream world behind him, slamming his fists repeatedly into the figure. With each blow, the pillar creaked and pulsed. All the while, Igneous remained stoic, as though he welcomed the attack.

"John, stop. You're breaking the pillar." Abby grabbed his arm as he reared back to take another swing. John let the shadows course through his body, and dance out on to his skin as a dark electrical current built up. A shock zapped Abby at his whim, knocking her away from him. He couldn't let Igneous get away with what he'd done.

John put every ounce of energy he could muster behind his swing. His mind reeled with the thoughts and feelings pent up inside him representing the bits and pieces of fear and anger carried by the shadows of the nightmares of others.

Imagination could be just as powerfully destructive as it was creative.

He swung. His momentum combined with the power of the shadows carried him forward even as the figure in front of him disappeared in a puff of smoke.

His knuckles slammed against the pillar, driving through with every ounce of shadow energy flowing into the monolith.

John knew he'd made a major mistake even before the blinding flash of light stunned him. The crack expanded around the circumference of the pillar, and the tall structure creaked in mock agony.

John directed his attention to the top of the pillar, where the structure swayed precariously. Like a large tree being chopped down in a forest, the monolith tipped slowly at first before breaking away from its base and picking up speed before slamming into the ground.

A ghostly laugh echoed as the shadows worked to reform the cloaked figure's body.

John couldn't bring himself to move, too worn out to comprehend.

Igneous rose up, appearing unharmed by John's blows. If anything, he came back bigger and stronger.

"John, watch out," Abby yelled.

John had barely a moment to throw his arms up to block as a barrage of shadow bullets peppered the shield that appeared around him. It was the same one Milo used to be able to throw up when channeling his bloodstone.

Igneous dove toward John and this time it was his turn to act as the weak prey about to be picked off. Three things happened simultaneously. John was knocked out of the way when Lily slammed into his side. Igneous changed into a blur as his attack hit Lily instead. An explosion of light flashed from the pillar, blinding John.

Chapter Eighteen

The ringing in John's ears refused to die down. The last thing he remembered was Lily pushing him out of the way before taking the brunt of the blow from Igneous as he tried to escape the dream world. The explosion. The blinding flash of light. It all had happened so fast.

A single image had burned itself into his memory, clear as day. Lily standing tall in front of the pillar. Her entire body radiating with power as she expelled Igneous from the dream world. The dream catcher had done exactly what she was supposed to do. She caught the nightmare and only let the good dreams escape. This thought brought a smile to John's face. Like waking up from a bad dream, he somehow knew everything was going to be okay.

Now, if only he knew where he was. One thing was certain; he was no longer inside a dream. He must be back in the hotel. In the dim light, he could just barely make out a pile of rubble around him.

This room. How did he get here? He recognized the curve of one of the larger pieces of statue, an arm extended out as though it were reaching out to him from the floor. Other statues, still intact, stood still in the silence.

Only one statue had been destroyed, and it must have taken considerable effort. A full powered blow from Mark's sharpened claws had done nothing to this statue earlier.

John couldn't say he was upset by the circumstances, especially if it meant Igneous could not be brought back. He had to get out of here, get back to his friends, and make sure they were okay.

John ran to the door and reached for the handle, but his hand passed straight through it. He stared, dumbfounded at his new development. Maybe he missed it? He tried again. This time he was convinced it wasn't a fluke. He couldn't feel the handle.

He pressed his hand up against the door, but didn't feel anything. Pushing through, he found himself in the hallway as though the door didn't exist as a barrier.

John's head was spinning. He needed answers. The hotel blurred around him and faded, the walls melting away. He could faintly make out Milo's voice and tried to concentrate on it. Even though he wasn't moving, the world around him shifted and changed, and he found himself back inside the labyrinth.

"It can't be too late. We have to get him back to the infirmary." Milo's voice was filled with concern. John slowly walked up behind them to figure out what they were talking about.

Pavlovian was huddled over John's body, a syringe poised in his hands. He blinked, unsure if what he was seeing was real. John's body lay unconscious in front of him.

"What the...?" he muttered in disbelief. Is this what people meant when they said they were having an out of body experience?

"Milo," he called out, trying to get his friend's attention. The others were a short distance away but nobody seemed capable of hearing him.

"We'll take him back to the infirmary and see if we can fix this there," Pavlovian said.

"I can't," Ruby said.

John blinked and the labyrinth was gone, replaced once again by the room full of statues. This was where he escaped the dream world.

"Am I dead?" John wondered. No, he refused to entertain the thought. But how could he explain not being able to touch anything? And nobody could see or hear him. Maybe he was a ghost?

A small jab in his arm sent a wave of pain through him. For a moment, the room grew cold. A tugging sensation gripped his chest, dragging him from the room. He was pulled out into the hallway, down the corridor, and into the infirmary.

He knew some time must have passed, but was unsure how much. Pavlovian and Milo, as well as Jade and Riley were hovering over one of the cots. A lone set of beeps echoed through the room. The rest of the machines were off, and the beds were empty. What he saw in the bed chilled him. It was his own body lying unconscious. How was this even possible? John came to a sobering conclusion. This wasn't just another dream he would wake up from. By going through the tower, he must have somehow separated from his physical body.

"Thank you, Milo, if it weren't for your help this past week I never would have been able to figure out the formula to break Felicia's hold." Pavlovian's voice was distant but distinct.

They did it. They stopped her. Despite his current situation, John couldn't help but feel a sense of relief.

"How did it work?" Milo asked. John latched onto his voice, using it as his anchor to this world, fearing he was still on the verge of accidentally slipping back into the dream.

"A lot like Nina actually. She was able to activate a person's pineal gland, kick-starting the production of melatonin...basically she caused the brain to think it was tired."

"Why didn't it work on him?" Milo asked. John felt a hand slide into his own, and he smiled. The warmth of Milo's phantom touch gave him a new strength.

"I'm not sure," Pavlovian spoke in a whisper, just barely high enough so John could pick up on what he was saying.

"Riley, first thing tomorrow morning I'd like you to go to your parents' diner. Tell them we need raw meat. That should hold over Mark and Ruby until they can get a proper meal." Pavlovian's order firmly represented his ability to understand their needs. He was keeping them safe and protected. John couldn't believe how easily Zack and Felicia had nearly convinced him otherwise.

John made his way into the room.

"John?" Milo blinked and ran over to him. Milo could see him. "What? How are you...?"

As desperately as he wanted to embrace Milo, he knew it would be impossible.

"I think I came out of the dream world the wrong way. Igneous was trying to escape but Lily stopped him." John looked over at his body on the bed. The neuro scan was going crazy, the patterns and colors shifting like oil inside a lava lamp.

"You're a shadow."

"I'm sorry. If I had trusted you, none of this would have happened." John lowered his head.

"It's okay. I can't say I gave you much reason to trust me. We'll figure this out. At least we're together again." Milo gave him an honest smile, and the heart monitor John was attached to started beeping like crazy. John felt his face heat.

He reached out for Milo and placed his hand on his friend's chest, expecting it to pass right through, but instead his body filled with an unnatural warmth. He pulled away as the heart monitor skipped the next beat.

The connection between them had lasted a mere instant, but it was strong and pure.

John's emotions were running so high all he wanted to do was take a moment and just rest his head on Milo's shoulder.

"Can we talk?" Milo smiled and pulled away from him. There were still many issues they needed to work through, but there would be time for that later. Igneous had been stopped.

"Can I borrow John?" Jade playfully stepped between the two of them and said, "Don't worry, Milo, I'll have him back before bedtime."

John felt a sense of pride in the way she stepped up. Instead of hiding behind her tough exterior, she finally admitted she needed help, and from him no less. Her form shimmered in front of his eyes, and he saw his friend clearly for the first time. To everyone else in the room she was the same old Jade, but he could see the truth. John saw Jayden for who he truly was.

"We will always be here for you, no matter what," John said with utmost sincerity. He mentally kicked himself for not being aware of Jayden's problems early on. Nobody should have to take on life alone, or go through their troubles thinking they can't rely on their friends. True strength comes from support and trust.

"Can you help me talk to my father?" Jayden was ready.

****

John and Milo spent the next couple of days in a holding pattern. Neither of them wanted to be the first to bring up the events of the past week. The fragile front they'd put up would be too easily shattered. John stared at the strange green stone on the nightstand between beds. He first saw the stone around Milo's neck before he was forced asleep in the labyrinth. Milo still hadn't mentioned anything about it.

John watched Milo button the top of his dress shirt, one he'd gotten especially for that day. The silence between them was deafening. John knew he was going to lose this game of chicken. He was never all that good at keeping things bottled up inside.

"Can we talk?" John sighed and took hold of his quartz. He could almost hear the shattering of the imaginary glass wall between them. He worried about how Milo would react, but when he smiled back at him, all the tension in John's body seemed to melt away.

"I wasn't sure you wanted to." Milo picked up the malachite and pulled the necklace over his head. The dark green of the gem paired well with his eyes.

"You should have talked to me from the very beginning." John wanted to be angry, but he was more tired than anything else. He hadn't had a restful night's sleep in days. Every time he tried to close his eyes, all he could see was the broken tower in the distance, and even though he knew it was over he couldn't help but feel as though they would always be waiting for Igneous' next attempt.

"I know. It was wrong to keep secrets. It's difficult for me to let people in, Pavlovian wasn't sure we were going to be able to find my true gem bond." Milo's hand rose to the malachite. John was having trouble wrapping his head around what Milo was saying.

"I thought your true bond was with a bloodstone." John knew the topic was a touchy one, but the only way they were going to air out everything between them was if they weren't afraid to talk.

"It wasn't. It was manufactured. When it was removed, I was no longer protected by Gem Haven, and at the same time, I was putting us in danger. Abby is a good tracker, but there are trackers on the other side as well. Gem Haven is designed to mask Lavalieres and I wasn't one."

"So Pavlovian helped you find that?" John pointed to the necklace, he hadn't ever heard of anyone bonding with multiple gemstones.

"That's where the lucid dream experiments came in. I learned a lot and we figured out that my bond was with malachite. I still don't know much about what powers it comes with, that's why I've been spending so much time alone. Everyone else already has their thing, and I didn't want to be part of that until I knew what my thing was." Milo came over and sat down next to John. "I'm sorry."

A pounding knock came at their door, and John felt his heart leap into his throat. He could only imagine how insane the lines of the heart monitor his physical body was hooked up to must have been.

"Hey invisible boy, are you coming? And make sure you bring John." Mark laughed out in the hallway while Milo and John shared a confused look.

"Get it? Because even though John's incorporeal now, you're the one who hasn't been around. Fine, never mind. Come on. Don't want to be late." Mark had already taken off, while the two of them rolled their eyes.

The courtyard had been transformed for the event. On both sides the team pillars stood tall, draped in gold and silver. John was happy to be able to be there with Milo by his side. This impromptu celebration had been called together by Pavlovian and the turnout was a lot greater than expected.

John could barely contain his excitement as they waited for Pavlovian to take his spot in the field. A single red throne was set up between the pillars and was meant for one specific person.

"I am proud of each and every one of you. We have had some difficult times lately, but I promise to do my best to keep you all safe here at Gem Haven. To me, you are all like my children." Pavlovian's voice rang out through the arena. As he spoke, the quiet conversations ceased and all eyes turned to him.

"Today is different. Today I get to honor my biological child with a proper Lavaliere ceremony. Please take your seat." Pavlovian paused.

A boy stepped out from behind the pillar, his features familiar, yet new. His hair had been buzzed short, and he looked a lot more comfortable in his new wardrobe. He took a seat on the throne. Everyone in the room was on their feet and clapping,

"I'd like to reintroduce my son, Jayden Pavlovian,

Son of Jade." Pavlovian pulled out a golden necklace and placed it around Jayden's neck. Jayden locked eyes with John and mouthed two words, *Thank you.*

A word about the author...

Nicholas began reading at the age of three, and not long after that, began writing as well. He found an interest in young adult fantasy early on and finished the first draft of his first full-length novel in 2006. Nicholas strives to write at least one full length novel each year and hopes to someday be a household name...in the houses of his friends and family at the very least.